Romans by Paul

The Apostle's Defense of Catholic Doctrine

By Richard L. Akins

En Route Books and Media, LLC
Saint Louis, MO

⊕ENROUTE
Make the time

En Route Books and Media, LLC

5705 Rhodes Avenue

St. Louis, MO 63109

Cover credit: Dr. Sebastian Mahfood, OP

Library of Congress Control Number: 2021934689

ISBN-13: 978-1-952464-67-6

Nihil Obstat

Censor Deputatus

October 29, 2015

Permission to Publish

Most Reverend Joseph M. Siegel, D.D., S.T.L.

Vicar General, Diocese of Joliet, October 29, 2015

<u>Dedication</u>

To my parents, Ann and Dick Akins

Table of Contents

Chapter 1: The Foundation 1

Chapter 2: The Only's 15

Chapter 3: The Five Points 31

Chapter 4: The Structure of Romans 61

Chapter 5: From the Beginning 91

Chapter 6: Young Catholic Eyes 127

Chapter 7: Taking a Breath 143

Chapter 8: A Cloud of Witnesses 153

Chapter 9: Romans 10-15 171

Chapter 10: Jesus Speaks 183

Chapter 11: The Parables of Calvin 207

Chapter 12: The Five Attributes 239

Chapter 13: A Flowering Faith 255

Selected References 263

Chapter 1

The Foundation

God is unfair.

The thought rolled through my mind like a tsunami. Born and raised Catholic, I listened consistently to several Evangelical Christian preachers while driving to and from work. For nearly five years (at the point when this troubling thought became clear), I also attended a pair of Evangelical churches every other weekend, alternating with Catholic Mass.

At first, maybe because I was hearing old Christian stories told through a new set of voices, the preaching was encouraging and exciting. But I realized as I heard the occasional anti-Catholic sermon, I had to make a choice. For my own sake and that of my children, I had to decide the future direction of my Christian life based upon more than a gut emotional feeling, and upon more than the decision to simply stay in lockstep with my family's traditions.

I understood that the official teaching of the Catholic Church holds that baptized Protestants are part of Christ's family, even if they do not practice the fullest expression of our Catholic faith. The form of Evangelicalism I was personally exposed to, however, does not believe Catholics are saved. These 'Evangelicals'[A] believe in what I call Predestined Individual Election (PIE), and I came to recognize that this belief system unfortunately paints for us a picture of an unfair God.

Not all Protestants who consider themselves to be 'Evangelical' share in the views of the churches I've attended. However, I know from personal and sometimes painful experience that those Christians who do follow this doctrine are the most vocal and aggressive in their attempts to 'convert' Catholics and even 'mainline' Protestants. They view this effort as a moral imperative, for they do not consider this conversion as disrupting the faith of other true Christian believers. Instead, they assume they are bringing to Christ those who follow a false path, a false gospel. While I do not wish to offend other Evangelicals, for brevity's sake I will refer to these Christians, who often call themselves 'Reformed' or 'Calvinists,' as 'Evangelicals' within this book.

Recently, I became deeply involved in the work of ecumenism – interacting with non-Catholic Christians with the goal of generating greater unity. As with any relationship, success in this area requires willing hearts on both sides. Fortunately, much progress has been made with Christians from various walks of life, particularly Orthodox, Lutherans and the like. However, ecumenism remains a difficult path between Catholics and Evangelicals.

In his document *The Ecumenical/Interreligious Office and*

the Diocesan Commission, Father Don Rooney summarized the ecumenical work being done with various Christian denominations. He writes, 'In the U.S., there have been no formal discussions between these two (Catholic and Evangelical) groups.' Part of the reason is that 'One of the obstacles to discussions with Evangelicals is the lack of a distinct ecclesial policy' (in other words, there is no central, consistent Evangelical 'church' to deal with).

This may be true, but in my experience, the more pressing problem is that, for many Evangelicals, interactions with Catholics are not considered ecumenical in the first place. These efforts are seen more in line with 'inter-faith' dialogue since many Evangelicals do not believe Catholics follow a faithful Christian understanding of the gospel. To accomplish anything in terms of ecumenical outreach, we Catholics need not only to better understand our Evangelical brethren, but also grow in knowledge with regard to the specific biblical tenants that lie at the foundation of their professed faith.

And, for Catholics like me who suddenly face claims that they, or their children, are not really Christian and that they need to abandon the faith and convert, these challenges must be addressed through a logical review of both the Bible and the Apostolic faith as a whole.

For the Catholic reader, we will discover the basis for this divisive view that we are not Christian and understand the precise biblical explanations as to why this conclusion is false. For the lay Catholic and clergy alike, we must expose ourselves to the specific accusations of our fellow Christians and understand how to answer them effectively before we, our family and our friends, are challenged. These challenges often come from not just self-identified Evangelical communities, but also from congregants of 'Bible' churches who themselves sometimes don't realize their expression of Christianity is based upon Calvinism.[B]

For my Evangelical brothers and sisters, we will discover how the divisive portions of the Evangelical faith hamper the goals of our Lord. We can sincerely seek to rebuild trust within the family of Christ and pursue the common goals of all Christ-followers. We must look at the scriptures with open eyes to understand the true meanings of the biblical writers. Then, we can strive together toward our eternal reward while building the Kingdom of God within our world today.

1.1 Uneasy as PIE

To summarize what we will soon discuss in detail, the set of Evangelical doctrines I bring together below as a Predestined Individual Election (PIE) claim that God chooses certain individuals, from all eternity past, to receive and possess faith in Christ. Due to the faith he has given only to them as individuals, they are 'elected' to eternal salvation. Some of us, personally and individually, are therefore 'predestined' to be considered one of God's 'elect'. This election is not conditional upon anything we do, or say, or think. Instead, a few of us will be changed, to our very core natures, through 'regeneration,' which forces us not only to want God, but to want him irresistibly.

At the same time, those whom God did not choose for election are predestined for damnation. These individuals are considered 'reprobate'. They are those who cannot, by their very nature, desire anything of God, nor take a single step toward him. Those who suffer this fate, ending in eternal torment in hell, were not rejected for anything they said, did, or thought. Their damnation is due only to the sovereign choice of the Creator.

1.2 The Seeds

As I attended a decade's worth of Evangelical services, this doctrine of PIE gnawed at me, due to its apparent unfairness. On the radio, on the Internet, and in person, I listened to more and more Evangelical pastors explain their own coming-to-faith struggles. Many, if not most, shared these same doubts regarding fairness. In time, however, they each succumbed to the decision to simply believe this doctrine, assuming it represented the only possible biblical truth.

However, if PIE theology is wrong, then it is not God who is being unfair to us, but these same Evangelicals who are being unfair to their fellow Christians. If PIE is in error, so is the use of this doctrine as a litmus test between those considered to be true Christians and all others who would be considered unsaved and, ultimately, enemies of God.

I have truly learned much from both my Evangelical and Catholic experiences. I did not approach the subject of finding 'true Christianity' from a negative point of view toward either of these Christian traditions. I am merely a father of three, concerned about the spiritual upbringing of my children, trying to answer what surely are many difficult questions. We will investigate in these pages whether the interpretation of specific points in scripture used by those with a divisive and exclusive view of our Christian faith may not be the *only* (or even the *correct*) understanding with respect to what God, through the writers of the New Testament, has conveyed to us.

There is some divergence among the Evangelical community, so I am not claiming all Protestants, or even all Evangelicals, believe in all aspects of PIE exactly as we will define it. Evangelicals sometimes allow even relatively small differences to damage their own church unity. It is an undeniable fact that the first Protestant movement centuries ago has spawned literally thousands of denominations and independent congregations. Some are divided over baptism, some over the reading of the book of Revelation and the end times, others concerning the differences between more liturgical faith practices and those who are 'free-form'.

However, most follow the tenets of the 16th-Century Protestant leader, John Calvin. Most are sincere in their faith and, like all Christians, have been brought up within a single faith family, with a specific reading of various sections of the Bible. They share in a foundational faith tradition that came out of the 1500-1700s, defined by such documents as the West- minster Confession and decisions from the Synod of Dort.

The most important set of Evangelical doctrines – the so- called 'Doctrines of Grace' - is abbreviated by the acronym 'TULIP'. To make the urgency of this book and our discus- sions make sense, this flower is where we need to start.

1.3 TULIP

The two primary issues the early Protestant Reformers (in the 1500s) viewed as core to their protest against Catholicism were 'Sola Scriptura' and 'Sola Fide' (salvation through the Bible alone, and salvation through Faith alone).

In today's world, however, the true dividing line from the Evangelical point of view revolves around a person's belief in a specific 'Gospel'. In their view of Christ's 'good news,' the foundational doctrines of *predestination* and *election* are used to call into question the 'Christian-ness' of non-Evangelicals. Predestination in this context holds that all of us have been chosen for our eternal fates by God. Election means that a portion of humanity, individually, is God's chosen ones, the elect. These people are individually predestined for heaven and heaven alone, with no possibility of failure. This predetermined *election* has nothing to do with us as individuals, it is due only to the Sovereign Will of God.

Anyone who doesn't follow the Evangelical faith is considered a member of the irredeemable group of individuals chosen from all eternity to be lost, damned to hell - the 'reprobate' of God. Catholics fit into this category, justifying for Evangelicals their challenges and conversion tactics 'in order to save our souls'.

Five corollaries, sometimes referred to as the 'Doctrines of Grace', further explain the Evangelical concepts of 'predestination' and 'election'. These are known by the acronym, 'TULIP', which stands for **T**otal Depravity, **U**nconditional Election, **L**imited Atonement, **I**rresistible Grace, and the **P**reservation (or **P**erseverance) of the Saints.

To put TULIP into simpler language, Evangelicals believe that they, along with the rest of humanity, are born completely lost; sinful and *totally depraved* individuals. This belief is of vital importance because it leads to their view that we humans live in a position of total dependence upon God and his unmerited grace alone for our ultimate salvation. They believe we are spiritually *dead* and therefore have no desire or ability to take even the first small step toward God in response to his call to faith. It is God's movement alone within our hearts that determines our fate, and he is totally responsible for whether or not we become and remain saved or unsaved.

Once the idea of Total Depravity is understood, the only explanation for why one person is saved by God and another person is damned, when that salvation is 100% dependent upon God and his actions alone, is that the saved individuals have been elected (chosen by God) to their individual salvation while all others who are unsaved are chosen by God to be damned. But this election itself cannot be determined by anything that we *are* or *do* or *say* or *think* prior to, or following, our justification and salvation. Therefore, those who are saved are said to have been Predestined for that salvation by God through nothing but his Sovereign Will. Since, in their view, none of God's decisions can change, our individual election must have been determined from all eternity past.

If one believes in this initial concept along the path toward Predestined Individual Election, then through the process of systematic thought and various hand-picked scriptural evidences, the other four points of TULIP represent one quite logical (but not exclusive or required) train of thought.

As we will discuss in more detail, if our justification comes from nothing we are or do, think, or say, then Grace is given to some of us *unconditionally.* Since the grace is not given to all people, then the atonement gained by the elect is *limited* only to a one small group of individuals. Since God has deemed some destined for salvation and he is all-powerful, the grace the elect receive, of course, must be *irresistible.* And, since the result of this grace is eternal salvation that has been predetermined by an all-powerful God, there is no possible way his determinations can fail, so those who are elected – the 'saints' – will be *preserved* in their faith throughout their lifetimes.

TULIP is not an illogical or evil belief system, and those who believe it can still be considered Christian and may be savable but, as we will see, TULIP may simply be based upon erroneous assumptions and the misreading of scripture.

From my personal reflections, the greatest failing with this theology is that it requires that God is utterly arbitrary and unfair. I have sat through numerous sermons at Evangelical churches and listened to hundreds of talks on the radio/Internet about this subject. In almost every case, the Evangelical preacher prefaces his talk by mentioning that a lot of people find these doctrines unfair at first. The explanation to this, however, is that 'God is God' and he makes the rules, and everything and everyone are subject to his will. Regardless of his decision to do one thing or another for each of us individually, to elect or not to elect us, his decisions are to be considered fair since, by definition, whatever he wills *is* fair.

And how do we know what his will is? According to those from the Evangelical tradition, we know God's will *only* because we read about it *only* in the Holy Scriptures. In other words, Evangelicals believe in the 16th century idea of '*Sola Scriptura,*' which is a fancy Latin term meaning, 'scripture alone'. They believe that if they read and interpret the Bible as supporting this group of doctrines I've summarized as Predestined Individual Election, then their interpretation of Holy Scripture trumps any emotion or thought or line of reasoning or logic we might bring to this issue. If scripture proves PIE is true, they believe we must accept this as reality;

both correct and fair.

However, during his trial at the Diet of Worms in 1521, the instigator of the Reformation, Martin Luther, proclaimed he had two guides for changing his mind concerning Christian doctrines – "If, then, I am not convinced by proof from Holy scripture, *or by cogent reasons*"[1] (other translations state this as 'evident reason'). When dealing with PIE, however, I have found many in the Evangelical faith ready to accept what he or she believes is derived from a specific interpretation of a set of scriptures, even at the expense of, or in conflict with, evident or cogent reason. In the remainder of this book, let us dive into the scriptures and see if we can derive from them an alternative, and possibly a more cogent and evident interpretation of the foundational truths of our Christian faith.

If the driving concept held by some Christians is that only their group of like-minded individuals are the 'elect' of God, and not only the elect but those predestined for election from all eternity past, the practical outcome is to then consider those who don't believe exactly the same way as being *hopelessly* unsaved. Eternally chosen for damnation by God. Reprobates who have been preselected to continue in hatred toward the Lord.

What other argument can make two groups of Christ followers more at odds with each other than for one group to believe the other is not only destined for hell, but has been chosen for this fate simply because God arbitrarily desired that outcome and wanted it from the beginning of time?

But what if *evident reason* and scriptures demonstrate a truth far different than Predestined Individual Election? What happens if there is an equally valid interpretation of scripture that points us away from the concept that God forced an eternal plan upon the world to save (or not to save) each individual person, without regard to what that person does, says, or thinks? What happens if *both* evident reason *and* the scriptures supports a Christian truth which is more inclusive of all those who call Jesus 'Lord and Savior'? A view that is more universal, more 'catholic'? Can we as brother and sister Christians then consider each other as sharing similar paths, all struggling toward our hoped-for eternity heaven with our God?

From my upbringing in the Catholic faith, and my more and more intense reading of scripture with specific Evangelical references in mind, I find widespread support for the idea that Christ came as a sacrifice for the whole world, not just some small group of elected individuals. Christ repeatedly calls upon all of us, as did Saint John the Baptist and the Old Testament prophets, to come before God in an attitude of true repentance, to choose to change our lives, to work with the grace of Almighty God.

The concept of repentance throughout scripture clearly has within it the call for us to do something, for us to make a decision, for us (in the words of Jesus himself) to *seek*, to *knock*, and hopefully, eventually to *find*. If there has been placed upon all of us a command to do something in cooperation with God's grace, there is just as clearly the opportunity for us to choose not to follow this heaven-sent path; to refuse to knock, to refuse to seek; to refuse to accept and, ultimately, to not find. Neither the elect nor the reprobate is eternally fixed upon their paths. We are all offered the opportunity, and the responsibility, to obey the Lord. To, as he said, love him.

1.4 Romans

Evangelicals believe their concept of individual election is supported in many areas of the New Testament, often in the writings of St. Paul, and most specifically within the Book of Romans. It was therefore with some trepidation, but also excitement and curiosity, that I spent a great deal of time researching the Evangelicals interpretation of Paul's words to those in Rome. I did not begin the study with an Evangelical mindset firmly in place, however, striving to read into specific passages just one interpretation. Neither was I a student trying to force a 'Catholic' theology upon the words of the Apostle.

Instead, I tried to search for the correct path from both the words on the page and an evidently reasonable understanding of who God is. In this quest, I was comforted in knowing that there is little in the idea of Predestined Individual Election, if true, that would strike at the very core of my own Catholic faith. In fact, some of the great Catholic theologians of the past strayed a few steps (or more) down some of the paths tread by today's Calvinist.

But, might another path open before us within that Book of Romans, and elsewhere, which provide an equally valid but different interpretation of what God wants to teach? In other words, is there some theological thread in Romans that Paul systematically laid out which does not require a strict belief in Predestined Individual Election? If there is, that by itself does not imply that Evangelical Christianity is entirely wrong – in fact, that was and is not my purpose at all - but it certainly throws into doubt the idea that their group of Christians should look at any other group of Christian individuals as being automatically unsaved.

If PIE can be shown to be at least not the ONLY acceptable biblical interpretation, we should then redouble our efforts to build bridges between our Christian families. We can reject the tendency to see each other as outsiders or enemies and instead embrace one another as sincere brothers and sisters of Christ. We would then present a more unified Christian lifestyle and Christian theology to the outside world of unbelievers, a Christian belief system that avoids concepts many consider inherently unfair. Finally, if we understand none of us are individually and eternally chosen by God, we will be motivated by our ongoing need to repent. We will make the daily decision to come back to the Lord by living more holy and pleasing-to-God lives.

Chapter 2

The Only's

While I tried to live as a faithful Catholic and Christ follower, my faith life was challenged in ways I did not expect (good and bad) during my time within Evangelical communities. I found myself as a parent forced into defending and explaining the Catholic faith in which I had brought up my children. Unfortunately, my education as a Catholic to that point in my life did not include a detailed study into what these challenges were, or how to respond to them. I knew that I was faithful, sincerely loved and wanted to serve the Lord, and yet I was faced with misunderstandings from other Christ followers on subjects such as the Catholic understanding of the role of Mary, or the doctrine of purgatory.

While we could dive into these subjects here, the details about those two specific issues are in Appendix A at the end of this book for those who are interested. The rest of this book, however, will deal with the various understandings of the process for our individual and communal salvation. The 'how' and 'why' of who we are as brothers and sisters of Christ.

But as a Catholic, I also realize that there was a time 500 years ago when a group of Catholics broke away from the church. While the rationale for Martin Luther's protest may have differed from those of other early Reformation leaders such as John Calvin, the one unifying issue between what would become the Protestant churches was the distrust of the Catholic Church. Obviously, those proposing to Catholics that they leave the church of their parents and grandparents and society as a whole needed support for this decision.

Over time, there developed essentially what became slogans for the Reformation. Shorthand descriptions of why the Reformers broke away from the church. These slogans didn't as much distinguish the various understandings of salvation but described the 'what' which distinguished one Christian faith community from the other. 'What' was the source of our recognized authority, 'what' were the goals of our faith lives, and 'what' did God provide in terms of our salvation.

While we will touch upon these understandings in their historical context, it is more important to see how these differences play out in world today. Not only can a modern reflection support Catholics in their faith, but a clear present-day understanding (separated from the passions of the early Reformation) may bring Christ followers toward unity again.

2.1 The Power of Five

The slogans employed by the early Reformation leaders and theologians have come down to us known as the 'solas,' a Latin term meaning 'only' or 'alone'. Some Protestants may argue that there were only two solas at the beginning, some may argue three, others point to the common listing today that there were five solas.

Now Catholics might bring up the argument, 'How can you say there is something that is the 'only' thing and yet have five of them?'

To be fair, this is a misunderstanding of the use of the term Sola. I can say, correctly, that I am alive today because the lungs 'alone' process oxygen and at the same time correctly claim that I am alive today solely because my heart pumps the blood. Two solas, acting together, that maintain my life.

To begin with, then, let's look at Solus Christus – Christ alone - and Soli Deo Gloria (for the Glory of God alone). At the time of the Reformation, Martin Luther and others could point at the glorious cathedrals of the Catholic church, including the new St. Peter's in Rome, and argue, "Those Catholics are not giving glory to God, they are building these edifices to glorify themselves and the Catholic church." In a similar way, they made the accusation that Catholics did not have faith in Christ alone, but instead in the Vicar of Christ, the Pope, and the rest of the clergy.

A third sola was called Sola Gratia. Grace alone. Here, the argument was that Catholics believe God owed them salvation because they faithfully carried out the commands of the Catholic church, whether it be the performance of good works or the celebration of the sacraments. The Reformers' argument was that God's salvation was granted to the chosen ones by God's grace alone, having nothing to do with anything that we did. Salvation was not earned; it was mercifully provided to some on an individual basis.

Those of us who are Catholic can see clearly how these three solos should no longer be issues brought up as challenges to the faith. The Catholic Church does not teach that God owes us salvation. For even if God created the same type of intricate ceremonial laws that he did for the Jews in the Old Testament, that law itself would be given to us not because God owed us but because God is mercifully and graciously pouring out his love upon us. Everything Catholics do and everything Catholics hope for in terms of heaven above is only available to us because of the grace of God.

For those who argue that Sola Christus should be used to divide Christ followers between true believers and false believers, the simple question is, 'Who else but Jesus Christ is seen by Catholics and either Savior or Lord?' Even the Pope, the Vicar of Christ, does not derive respect and veneration for himself, but only due to his role in leading Christ's church in succession of the Apostle Jesus placed in leadership over the infant faith.

Finally, though we fallible human beings rarely meet the standard, what else is there in Catholic life more important than giving glory to God? The artwork and architecture, music and theology, science and literature found within the Catholic mind is, in idea at least, created for the glory of the Father, the Son, and the Holy Spirit.

2.2 Fide

It is here that we reach the first of two points that can rightly be seen as still dividing Protestants and Catholics. 'Sola fide.' Faith alone.

We can all imagine when the first generation of Reformed preachers placed themselves at odds with the Catholic Church following fifteen hundred years of Christian theological and ecclesiastical (relating to the church) development. How many of their perspective converts asked the simple question, 'What are we supposed to do?'

The only answer for the Reformers was that there was no answer. For what individual or groups of individuals in the sixteenth century could suddenly claim, 'We discovered practices which are better'?

No, the only effective response was that no practices and no sacraments and no activities of the church could have any impact on our individual salvation. Salvation could only come through faith; the specific faith being proposed by the Reformers themselves.

And yet, belief in 'salvation through faith alone,' since it questions any and all actions on our part, can lead to an understanding that our ongoing sins no longer matter. That all sins (past, present, and future) are already forgiven for anyone who follows Evangelical beliefs. Beyond the biblical texts to the contrary, which we will detail later, this 'faith alone' concept can lead to what many call 'cheap grace'. The problem is put very well by a decided anti-Catholic Evangelical preacher, John MacArthur, in his book <u>The Gospel According to Jesus</u>:

> The church's witness to the world has been sacrificed on the altar of cheap grace.... They have been told that the only criterion for salvation is knowing and believing some basic facts about Christ. They hear from the beginning that obedience is optional. It follows logically, then, that someone's one-time profession of faith is more valid than the evidence of that person's ongoing lifestyle in determining whether to embrace him or her as a true believer.[2]

This is what we will address in the remainder of this book. One of our tasks is to investigate if a feeling alone, a specific faith without obedience or action, is all we need to come to, and remain, with Jesus Christ our Lord and Savior in eternity.

2.3 Sola Scriptura

This, then, brings us the last of our Five Solas, Sola Scriptura, or 'scripture alone'. For it will only be effective for us if we speak about faith alone through the only 'language' acceptable to those who often divide the faithful. The language of the biblical texts.

To be fair, Sola Scriptura is sometimes misunderstood by Protestants and Catholics alike to mean a 'literal' reading of the biblical texts. Since different people can understand the literal meaning of the same words or phrases differently (not to mention the fact that the interpreters who write our Bibles in modern languages can disagree), most Protestants will look to the Church Fathers and other theologians to help decipher the meaning of the texts.

Sola Scriptura, then, means that nothing in our faith lives can be believed or take place which is not explicitly in scripture. More specifically, everything needed for our salvation is to be found in the Bible. Using this definition, Evangelicals argue that Catholics are forced to believe in concepts (such as the bodily assumption of Mary) which are extra-biblical and therefore false.

Two things are clearly in the Bible, however. First, Jesus established his Church upon the Apostles. Second, he gave them and their successors the guidance and authority of the Holy Spirit to 'loose' and to 'bind'. When they, for example, formally determined the doctrine of the Trinity (which is, of course, also supported by scriptures), acceptance of this official dogma, or rebellion against it, affects our individual futures with God.

So, in brief, what do Catholics believe concerning the Bible? A great deal is written in the Catechism about scripture. With an eye toward the Evangelical distrust I have witnessed firsthand, I find the following paragraph to be most helpful:

> Read the scripture within "the living Tradition of the whole Church". According to a saying of the Fathers, Sacred scripture is written principally in the Church's heart rather than in documents and records, for the Church carries in her Tradition the living memorial of God's Word, and it is the Holy Spirit who gives her the spiritual interpretation of the scripture (CCC, Paragraph 113).

To my Evangelical friends, I also point out that the New Testament was written (from a human standpoint) by members of what would develop into the formal Catholic Church (John was a bishop, James was a bishop, Paul set up churches following the oral teachings of the first Apostles, and Peter was the first of what would become the 'Popes' of the Catholic faith). For the first three hundred years of Christian history, most people within the Christian Church were baptized as Catholics do today, understood the sacraments and Mass as Catholics do today, and studied the writings that would later be defined by Catholic leadership as the New Testament. Under the guidance of the Holy Spirit in the fourth century, various Catholic Councils and synods settled many thorny theological issues. From their decisions, we have the foundational Christian beliefs (Trinity, etc.) believed by nearly all modern Christians.

Still, there remains an active argument, centuries old, that essentially teaches, 'Catholics hate the Bible.' That the Catholic Church once banned and burned the scriptures. That the Church refused to let everyday Catholics read the Holy Writ.

Now, let's think for a moment about this issue. Do we simply hand out a bunch of medical books the first day of Pre-Med studies and let the students read the books on their own to learn their craft? I was educated as an engineer, and had highly trained professionals lead every class, guiding our instruction even down to a slide which taught the obvious fact that, 'That which is non-linear, is not linear." This is the world of higher education, even though most engineering and medical and legal students today are highly literate and come into school with top-notch educations.

With that in mind, what was the Church to do in the Middle Ages when the vast majority of potential Bible readers couldn't read at all?

Today's Catholics, like myself, do study the Bible. The Catholic Church loves the Bible. Every Catholic, in fact, hears two or three separate readings from the Bible at every Mass. Every three years those readings cover 72% of the New Testament, roughly 3,300 verses from the Old Testament, and a whopping 90% of the four Gospels.[3] In fact, the Catechism exhorts all Catholics to immerse ourselves in scripture, properly read:

> The Church "forcefully and specifically exhorts all the Christian faithful... to learn the surpassing knowledge of Jesus Christ, by frequent reading of the divine scriptures. Ignorance of the scriptures is ignorance of Christ. (CCC, Paragraph 133)

But, and here is the key issue up to this point, Catholics do not believe the Bible can interpret itself. We know even three hundred years after Christ, and in full possession and use of the Biblical writings we now have, there was a large part of the church which denied that Jesus was divine. In fact, the founders of most of the major heresies, rejected by the Catholic, Orthodox, and Protestant churches, used the New Testament scriptures as their proof-texts as well. Further, it would appear evidently reasonable to reject the idea that the Holy Spirit guides us *individually* to *universal* truths using only the words of scripture. We have the real-world proof that this approach fails as we witness the spawning of literally thousands of Protestant denominations and independent Bible churches teaching slightly different universal biblical 'truths'.

When we do explore *universal* truths, we, as Catholics, believe these concepts have been handed down from Jesus himself through his first followers and down through the centuries through successive leaders of the Church. These are truths the Church's founders – the first Apostles and those who lived with Jesus – knew and passed on to their followers, the full spirit of which can hardly be put into words. How, for example, can any human adequately describe in writing the Resurrection of your friend (and now Lord)?

Why do we need an authority to interpret the Bible? Perhaps my father put it best, 'We are reading biographies of our Lord Jesus Christ, not an autobiography.'

We also remember that neither Jesus, our Lord and Savior, nor his Apostles, wrote a book prior to beginning the Church and spreading the faith. The Apostles and their successors were not led by the Holy Spirit to define a new canon of scripture for almost four hundred years.

We certainly study the Bible, but when there are areas of confusion or doubt, we take as our guide the collective wisdom of the Catholic Church, which has been inspired and protected through the centuries by the Holy Spirit. While this may not satisfy some adhering to a scripture "alone" concept of the Christian faith, I frankly don't see where any other Christian denomination follows a purely Sola Scriptura approach either.

As far back as Luther and Calvin, whenever there has been

a debate, such as happened concerning the Real Presence in the Eucharist, both sides went beyond the use of only the Bible to defend their points. Both sides debated the issues using the writings of the Church Fathers and their own personal experiences and reason. They, eventually, created various Protestant Traditions just as earlier Catholic debates added to the living Catholic Tradition. And, when Protestants needed to better define their belief systems, they also developed creeds and confessionals, such as the Augsburg Confession or the Heidelberg Catechism, just as the Catholic Church created the Creed at Nicaea and published the Catechism of the Catholic Church.

Now, to my brother and sister Catholics – do we truly understand what our Evangelical brethren are worried about regarding our Tradition? First, they naturally fear their interpretation that the Catholic Church's claims a monopoly on truth.

Second, when we say that truth is derived both from the written Word of God and from Tradition, what they fear is the Catholic Church suddenly making a claim like this; 'While the Bible says nothing about cats and dogs as household pets, there has always been a super-secret teaching from Jesus, handed down verbally to his Apostles and down through the ages, hidden within the Catholic Church to this very day. "We proclaim that dogs should be allowed in the family home, but cats are evil and should be banished to the wastelands."

The answer to this second concern is one of reassurance. Catholics fought and won the battles against the heresy of Gnosticism fifteen hundred years ago. We did not accept their idea of a 'secret knowledge' then, and we don't claim any type of secret knowledge now. As I've become more directly exposed to the Evangelical ideas of the Rapture, that is a good example of a 'hidden' knowledge, a hidden Tradition of sorts. For while there have always been end-of-the-world prophecies, the specific ideas of the Rapture as we know it today were not widely preached until the middle of the 1800s.

There is no similar hidden Catholic knowledge or interpretations of scripture which have surfaced for centuries, if not millennium. In fact, I'm confident that if there were any secret beliefs within an unwritten Tradition of the Catholic Church, like we are descendants of some alien race, that information would have come out by now. It would not have remained a secret for two thousand years. Our faith has faced every question that could possibly challenge a religious system. I can't imagine any new secret belief will spring to life. In fact, even when we discuss the early 'oral' traditions of the Church, we all understand that most of those traditions that concern our core theological beliefs eventually were written into the New Testament. Christ does not change, and neither do our beliefs about his life, death, and resurrection.

But while the Church does not change, something else does. The world. And this leads us to the value and *necessity* of our Tradition. Jesus knew quite well that his one Body needed one source of final authority.

When the world changes - for example with the advent of artificial insemination or human cloning in our own time and near future - our Churches must struggle with the morality of these activities. A truly 'Sola Scriptura' Evangelical would have very little to say about either case, for the Bible does not use the words artificial insemination or cloning. The Bible's silence on these issues would logically eliminate the Sola *Scripturist's* ability to make any moral arguments whatsoever.

In contrast, the Catholic faith can determine and teach correct morality not only from the Bible but also from the Tradition of the Church. We can claim the moral authority to state that the soul, for example, is a unique and precious thing, and cloning will create a wide range of potentially negative effects, many of which we can only guess about at this point. Since we place ultimate authority in the Church Christ founded, then the ongoing decisions of that Church are valid arguments in modern controversies.

If, to take another example, someone is to promote a certain level of respect for women, and we take a Sola Scriptura approach to the subject, reading texts written in a Middle Eastern culture two thousand years ago, we might (*might*) come up with some beliefs that place women into a subservient position.

However, the Catholic Church's 'Tradition' tells us that Christ, considering the time and place in which he lived, was shockingly welcoming to women. The writers of the New

Testament wrote about the issues between men and women in a much more 'modern' way than many of their secular contemporaries. The second most honored human being in the Catholic world is a woman. Several of the revered 'Doctors' of the Catholic Church are women. All this is a direct result and reflection of a love and respect for women found throughout the Catholic Tradition that may be considered by some 'extra-biblical'.

So, for my Evangelical friends, let me simply say this as we move into the following chapters. Most of what I will offer up for consideration will come directly from scripture. For we all love and respect the Holy Word of God, and I understand now better than ever that for many of you there is a deep need, prior to your acceptance of any new concept, for you to be convinced of Biblical support. But let us all understand that we *all* have and use Tradition as a framework for what we believe, and as a context for what we read.

2.4 Ecumenism

When I began writing this book, the goal was to explain what I and my family faced within our Evangelical experiences. During that time, I was involved with various events and activities directed toward 'ecumenism'. That is, the effort to build bridges between various expressions of the Christian faith.

I hope this book leads to greater ecumenical efforts on all

sides. What is more necessary in today's world than for the brothers and sisters of Christ to act like brothers and sisters?

Some may consider the topics and conclusion that follow to be challenging, at the very least, and perhaps even off-putting. The goal is not to insult any Christ follower, and certainly not to question anyone's love and faith among those who consider Jesus their Christ and Lord.

At the same time, this book is not asking to build unity within the family of Christ based upon a fake acceptance by those who truly believe others are not Christian in the first place. The book seeks to take a fresh look through scriptures, specifically using the sections of the Bible Evangelicals often use to support an 'exclusive' view of the faith. To understand – biblically – and accept that we are all called to the Father through Christ with the guidance of the Holy Spirit.

Chapter 3

The Five Points

There are several common approaches used by those who claim that Catholics (or mainstream Protestants) are not only not saved, but that we are unsavable. In the last chapter, we discussed the Five Solas affirmed by the Reformation. Slogans used for the last five hundred years to criticize the Catholic church and used to convert Christ-followers to other visions of Christian doctrines based upon what Christ did, and who God is.

In this chapter, we must return in detail to the items briefly described in our opening chapter, the Five Points of Calvinism. Not every Protestant is Calvinist, of course, but in my personal experience, those from this Christian tradition are the most likely to consider some Christians as not being Christ-followers at all, and therefore most likely to attack other believers to lead them away from their faith.

Calvinist views are necessarily entirely wrong. Calvinists themselves are certainly not evil. But, as we will see, their assumptions and actions are counterproductive at best, and deeply damaging to the family of Christ at worst. By holding to a set of beliefs which paints other Christians as being on the 'outside,' as being beyond the 'elect,' Evangelical thought purposefully creates distrust among members of Christ's family. The discussion of election and predestination also strikes many as presenting an image of an unfair God, thereby damaging our collective efforts to evangelize the broader culture. Finally, for those who follow these Reformed tenants, there come the difficult psychological point where they must believe many of those they loved are now forever damned to hell, a damnation due to the eternal arbitrary will of a Sovereign God.

We should consider, then, the root of this new theology summarized by TULIP. What did the first Reformers contend with psychologically when convincing themselves, and those who eventually would follow them, to leave the Church? They had to first convince individuals that they didn't have to *do things* to be saved. Specifically, they didn't need to do the things commanded by the Catholic Church.

Without the historical authentication for their new dogmas, the Reformers developed the idea that what was adequate for saving a person's soul was nothing more than an ethereal 'faith' in Christ. The first Protestant converts came from the ranks of men and women brought up by parents and grandparents and a culture in which the Catholic faith played the key part of salvation, and the Catholic Church was God's mouthpiece on earth. They were taught to believe in the sacraments and other practices and dictates of the faith.

To accomplish their goals, the Reformers emphasized that the activities of the Catholic Church were not only unneeded but threatened one's salvation. They had to, in fact, teach that none of us, nor the all-powerful Catholic Church, could add anything to our own righteousness in hope of salvation. Instead, they had to prove their new teachings were more appropriate and in-line with what Jesus wanted. They could not, in other words, simply say that they had discovered a new Way, or a new set of activities and practices and works to compete with the Catholic Church. They needed to show that there was no 'way,' no activities prescribed by any church, that could lead souls toward eternal union with God.

The first step, then, involved developing a theology that insisted we humans, and our actions, do nothing to cause or add to our ultimate justification. The reason is obvious, for it we are required to *do* anything then the question would be 'what' should we do? We could only at that point do what we personally believe is right or do what some outside authority told us was correct. That authority, when it came to spiritual issues, must be our respective churches. And if we look to a single church to define what we need to do for salvation, then in the Christian world the institution with the best claim on this position of authority was the Catholic Church.

Particularly at the time of the Reformation, consider Luther or one of his fellow Reformers meeting a prospective convert and saying, 'Of course you need to live your life a certain way, and that way includes believing in the Christ the

Catholic Church claims as its founder and head, but you *must* follow us instead of the Catholic Church because we know better the proper tasks and disciplines you need to adhere to.'

It would seem to most, of course, that the Catholic Church would have had a much better historical claim on spiritual authority. The only real way to make the Reformation work was to claim, "There is no specific way you need to live, nothing you have to do, you simply need to believe. In fact, your ability to 'just believe' is harmed by all the other things you are being taught to do. Catholics don't teach you to 'just believe,' and therefore they are leading you astray."

But, Luther's listener might then say, "How can you insist none of my prayers matter, how can you say my sacrifices to the church, my receiving of the Eucharist, my confession of sins....how can you say none of that matters?"

"It doesn't matter," the Reformers would eventually respond, "because nothing you do can ever please God. In fact, none of us have any desire to please him. We believe that the Book of Romans tells us that we are all spiritually dead. Paul wrote there, 'There is no one good, not even one." We have vile souls, so we really can't pray or do good deeds or serve the Lord. Neither we nor our church have anything to do with our salvation, for we are all individually and collectively depraved and at odds with God. If there was even a speck of light and goodness within you, then you could begin to cooperate with God's call, and the Church could develop activities that would help you along your way. But there isn't even a glimmer. You are depraved. Totally Depraved."

That, then, was the first step along the path toward 'TULIP'. The concept of Total Depravity. The idea that we cannot act in even the slightest way toward the goal of union with God and eternal salvation. The doctrine that our individual salvation, should it be provided to us, is completely and wholly the decision of God alone.

Once we come to believe in our own Total Depravity, then the question is, 'How then can I be saved?'

The only answer is, 'Through the Grace of God.' But, since we can do nothing to earn this grace (because our souls don't desire this grace or relationship with God), salvific grace can only be considered unconditional. God gives some individuals this grace due only to his own choice, and not because he set any conditions for us to meet or maintain. A Calvinist insists that we, in our natural state, cannot *desire* to meet any conditions set by God. If there is even a single person in a state of saving grace, then this Grace was given to that person by God, and it was given to them without conditions. And what is this Grace? A regenerated soul with a newfound desire and will to believe in Christ as savior.

If this doctrine of Unconditional Grace is true, we must take an honest look about us. We realize one thing immediately - while this regenerative grace may be given to some unconditionally, it is not provided universally. Not everyone becomes a believer and servant of Jesus. Not everyone is saved.

What this means is that Christ came and died so that only a few individuals would benefit from God's eternal grace. Jesus' atoning work on the Cross, then, is 'Limited.' Not only limited in its actuality, but limited in its potentiality to save. He died, but most never even have the potential to benefit from this sacrifice. For not one person already predestined for hell ever comes to faith through Jesus' sacrifice. For them, the potential of his death and resurrection is limited.

This doctrine is referred to as Limited Atonement, the 'L' in TULIP. The efficacy (effectiveness) of Christ's death is limited, even before the crucifixion took place. Limited by God himself who created the human soul totally depraved and predetermined the ultimate status of each individual soul.

Now, faced with this problematic doctrine (some Evangelicals call themselves 'Four Point' Calvinists in protest over this one part of TULIP), I've heard Evangelical preachers such as the those on Ligonier Ministries rephrase this issue as 'Definite' atonement. While the outcome is the same – only a small group of people ever enjoyed the possibility of atonement – the rationale behind this redefinition is instructive.

It took me a while to understand the underlying reason for this revision of terms, but it essentially goes like this: if we claim Christ died but we humans must respond through our human-wills to his call for faith and salvation, then there was a chance that no one would ever have responded to Christ's call. In fact, since we are all in a state of Total Depravity, then not only could we all reject Christ's call, but we all *would* reject Christ and his works.

Therefore, the argument goes, since God the Father did not want God the Son to sacrifice himself in vain, he planned from all eternity for a specific group of Totally Depraved humans to be given saving grace so they would positively and 'Definitely' receive atonement.

There are two interesting issues concerning this thought process. First, this theory reflects the all-or-nothing philosophy that infects much of Predestined Individual Election. If one person – let's say Peter or Paul – is called miraculously by God to fulfill a certain task, then *all* people are seen as similarly predestined for the life they lead and the choices they make. In contrast, should we claim that we have any true humanwill* in responding or rejecting God's call, then supposedly we are claiming *all* the glory and credit for ourselves and leaving nothing for our Creator.

(*Note – we will avoid in this book the term 'freewill', for some Christians view it as *only* meaning that our wills supersede God's divine will. We will instead use the term 'human-will')

So, in this case, if one assumes we have human-wills capable of responding to God's call, even in the slightest measure, and that God will then open the door in response and work within us through the process of sanctification, then of course at least one person in history will choose Christ. (In addition to, of course, Mary, whose Immaculate Conception takes care of this Calvinist worry in the first place by making sure her Son's incarnation atoned for at least one soul).

Second, to me at least, the idea that the Father is somehow honoring his Son by *forcing* people to believe in him does the exact opposite. It neuters the power of Christ's life, his teachings, his Crucifixion, and Resurrection. If the Father predetermined the elect and the reprobate long before the incarnation, and not one person who was non-elect ever came to faith upon hearing of Jesus, did Jesus really accomplish anything?

So, we are now beyond the halfway point of the TULIP acronym and in a very real sense we have gone as far as we need to go. At this point, Calvinism maintains that out of all of humanity there are a fortunate few who have been chosen by God to receive Limited Individual Atonement through individually provided Unconditional Grace which regenerates individual souls from Total Depravity.

Who are these fortunate few? They are, in the words of Reformed Calvinist theology, the 'elect.' How and why did God chose these individuals out of all of humanity? Since we are all supposedly born Totally Depraved, all hopelessly dead in our sinful natures, God alone must have made this choice for his own reasons alone, not because of anything we ever did, or felt, or said, or believed. He made this choice, as

Evangelicals like to say, through his own Sovereign Will and for his own Glory. And, since God is an eternal God, his plan for the salvation of the elect, and for those individuals counted among the elect, has also been eternal, determined from the beginning of time.

Still, to my Catholic ears, this plan of God seems inherently unfair and unjust, perhaps some of you have felt the same way as you read this description. But before we go any further, it is important for us to realize, especially those from a Catholic background, that our Evangelical brethren sincerely believe this theology is not only biblically supported, but that it alone honors God. From this sincere and God-fearing intent, perhaps we can build new and lasting bridges.

Foremost in Calvinist's minds is a deep humility before God. In this, they are correct for we must all both acknowledge our own fallen states and thank God for the sacrifice of his Son. Calvinists fear that if we believe anything we do, think, or say helps determine our eternal fates, then we will rely only upon our own actions, our own goodness, our own works, and by doing so lose our proper reliance upon Christ.

Tied to this is their belief that God is all powerful. If so, then how can any of us be allowed to make the most important decision of our lives, that of either accepting or rejecting salvation through Christ? God must have planned all this out for us, and our final membership either inside the group of the elect, or outside it, must be entirely in his hands, or he would not be all-powerful in the end.

These thoughts, and the first three Points of Calvinism, direct us then to the final two doctrines. By the time we get to Limited Atonement, there might not be any other logical outcome except to believe in Irresistible Grace and the Preservation of the Saints. Irresistible Grace means that if we are dead in our sins and incapable of making the slightest move toward God, then the grace some of us individually receive must come entirely and unconditionally from God. But would God be all-powerful if we human beings still then have the capacity to ignore or rebel against this grace? No. The grace he provides the elect must be Irresistible.

Finally, we come to the Perseverance (or, sometimes, 'preservation') of the Saints. This belief only makes sense if we make it as far as 'TULI'. If we are the children of an all-powerful God who has determined from the beginning of time that an individual is personally predestined to receive the saving grace of the elect, then God will not ever abandon us in our journey through life. 'Once saved, always saved' is the common phraseology, and all it really means is that if we are part of the elect, God will never change his mind about us and no other force in the universe can snatch us away from his loving embrace. He will Preserve us, and we will Persevere.

Now, I have heard at least a hundred sermons on this subject of TULIP and most of the pastors giving these sermons grudgingly acknowledge the seeming unfairness of these doctrines. For me, it seems obvious that if God predestined some of us individually for eternal salvation, he also chose the rest of humanity individually for eternal damnation. He created, in fact, billions of human souls that have no chance, regardless of what they ever did, knew, believed, tried, or succeeded at, to enjoy eternal salvation. To me, as much as I respected the Calvinists desire to protect the power, dignity, and sovereignty of God, their doctrines strike me as assaulting the loving, merciful, and just nature of our Lord.

Worse, it logically attacks the very reason for the birth, life, death, and resurrection of Christ. For if God already chose a set group of individuals to receive salvation, and the rest of us to receive damnation, and salvation has nothing to do with anything we do in our own lives, then you can see how Christ's life and sacrifice might be seen as meaningless. The Father might just as well choose his elect based upon the color of our eyes.

3.1 Dead in Sin

As I struggled to develop a coherent sequence of beliefs to explain the idea of Predestined Individual Election, I heard a certain analogy used several times. I could not find specific scriptural references from which the Evangelical preachers proposed this analogy, but the example at least provided a logical foundation for their broader beliefs.

This analogy plays to the very heart of the Calvinist world-view, that the glory for our salvation is to be given to God alone. This can only happen, seemingly, if we consider ourselves entirely powerless and therefore completely dependent upon God's grace. Like most of us, I realize that many times in my life I felt powerless against certain temptations or fears or doubts. Calvinists point to specific verses in scripture which they interpret to confirm that we are powerless and spiritually 'dead.' In other words, a person who is sick might cooperate with his doctor to help become healthier, but a dead person is just that, dead. If we are dead, then there is no hope for us, unless some other power steps in to resuscitate us.

Now, while we do read Paul state in the Bible that we are 'dead' in sin (Eph. 2:1), I always thought about the issue in terms of our experiences with a disease such as cancer. If I have a serious case of cancer, a doctor may tell me that I am 'dead,' meaning that if I don't follow his advice and make the correct choices in my treatment plan, my disease will certainly be fatal. Likewise, when the Apostle tells his readers that they are dead in their sins, I take this to mean that he is saying, 'Unless you make the right choices and follow the correct spiritual plan, you will be dead spiritually for eternity, due to your sins.'

Calvinists, on the other hand, take that word 'dead' in Paul's letters to mean just that, 'dead.' But that poses an interesting question, does it not? Why would Paul bother to write to those he considered dead, and therefore unable to fathom his meaning? Why would the Holy Spirit inspire the

Apostle to write words of warning if only the elect could ever hear and obey (and have no choice not to) while the pre-destined reprobate could never benefit?

There seems to be two options. Either Paul was describing us as being (without God's direct interference) dead. He was using 'dead' as a noun. A set reality. A state from which we have no choices since we have no human-will at all. We are in a state from which we will be revived, or not revived, only through the sovereign actions of God.

Or, Paul used his word, 'dead,' as an admonition. A warning against an unflinching future reality we would each face should we not respond to God's call and make at least the first small steps toward Christ.

In the Evangelical world, there is and always will be great difficulty explaining the reality that there are Christians who do fall away from the faith. Within the Catholic world, this is not only *not* difficult to explain, this type of 'backsliding' is expected. While we believe without God there is nothing we can do which will force him to save us, no set of rules or laws we can follow without faith and repentance to pry open the gates of heaven, we also understand that we have the God-given freedom to accept or reject his offer of salvation. We believe through first-hand knowledge and experience that God's call continues throughout our lives, and our correct, God-centered choices, likewise, need to be repeated through-out our lives as well. So, when some fail to make the correct choices and fall away from the faith, we don't see that as either a failure of God or as a failure in our theology. It is merely an expression of misused human-will.

But for Evangelicals who follow the general tenants of TULIP, the reality of fallen believers is a major problem. Remember, we are told that we are all dead in sin and incapable of any response at all to that small voice God puts within each of us. Every person who seems to possess the Christian faith therefore does so entirely because God regenerated their souls and gave them this saving faith. Since God is all-powerful, these new saints must be preserved in their faith to the end. A backslider could never, theoretically, have ever made a Christian proclamation for themselves without God's interference (for they are Totally Depraved), but within all whom God does interfere, he must do so irresistibly and permanently.

Where, then, come thou, O backslider?

Equally troubling for me is a similar challenge to Calvinism, 'What about the man or woman who has never heard about Christ?'

I am not at this stage speaking about the spiritual life-after-death experience of those who have never had the chance to learn about the Savior. The issue here is - we all see people who are not Christian, whether in our daily lives or half a world away through television or the Internet, who nonetheless at least try to live 'good' lives. The Buddhist monk who attempts to respond to the call for a spiritual connection with a higher power within his soul; the Afghan peasant who aides a fallen American soldier; the professed atheist who sends money to the people ravished by a typhoon; the billions of parents who sacrifice for the good of their children.

Are we to believe these people are all Totally Depraved? Many of them do the good that they do in a sincere hope to serve a 'god,' even if that god is not specifically the triune God of the Christian. And, just to be clear, the Calvinist definition of Total Depravity is not that we are all as evil as possible. It is simply that not one of us has any natural inclination to seek out, accept, or follow God.

But do not our eyes show us that most people have a basic goodness within them? Has not at least one human being we've met demonstrated a spark of God in their souls? Do not most of our acquaintances seem to respond the best way they can with their limited knowledge, to his call?

Or does everyone we know truly seem to be spiritually 'dead'?

More to the point of this book – did not Paul in the Book of Romans write that everyone has been given knowledge and wisdom by God, and therefore none of us have an excuse for our sins?

> …since what may be known about God is plain to them, because God has made it plain to them. For since the creation of the world God's invisible qualities—his eternal power and divine nature—have been clearly seen, being understood from what has

been made, so that people are without excuse. (Rom 1:19-20)

Paul reminds us that we all suffer from some level of spiritual sickness. Many of us might be spiritually ignorant about the details of Christianity, but God has made his basic rules 'plain to them.' We are all therefore responsible to make the right choices according to the law God placed within each of our hearts. If God did not provide this knowledge or created us in such a way that we could not follow and obey, then we would of course have a *perfect excuse.* But Paul confirms otherwise, we have no excuse.

Our birth under the curse of Total Depravity would be our just excuse. Since we have no excuse, we simply cannot be born in this totally depraved state.

3.2 What About Human-will?

I opened this book with the startling statement that God is unfair. The idea that God predetermines each individual's eternal salvation or damnation seemed to me obviously arbitrary long before I understood the Five Points of Calvinist. From my earliest days in the Evangelical world, I had another reaction to the new theology I was exposed to. I perceived immediately that this worldview was also an attack upon the concept of the human will.

Now, it is often the argument from Evangelicals that those

who believe in human-will must believe only in complete and totally free human will. Further, that if you believe in free human will then you must in turn reject all of God's Will, his plan, and his sovereignty. But that is not the case. God can and does move within us. Sometimes, and for certain people and purposes, he interrupts our world in a 'miraculous' way. But he has also made us in his image, with some level of freedom, through which we can believe and do, or reject to not do, those things which will bring us to eternal life.

That said, if you ask most Evangelical preachers, I believe they will insist their theology is amenable to human freedom. For a long while, I didn't understand how they held that belief when at the same time professing God directs our every thought, move, and action. So, it may be helpful here to lay out a common argument I have learned in this regard.

The outlook is basically this; Adam and Eve fell, and through the Fall we have all become Totally Depraved (as we described above). In other words, we are all now totally lost and do not have the slightest desire or capability to follow or seek God.

The next step, then, is the key.

If we are totally depraved morally and our very natures hate God and reject him, then we *can* have free will and *could* choose either good or evil, but we *only will,* by our very natures, choose evil. In other words, think of it like a man who was lean and healthy and then suffered a terrible car accident. This man is recovering for six months and began to gorge himself, putting on 100 pounds of weight. He now has a size 48 waist. One day, he finally is healed enough to get out of bed and waddle to his closet. Hanging before this man is a size 48 pair of pants, and next to it hangs the size 32 pants he used to wear before the accident. This man is perfectly free to choose to wear either pant, but he *only will* choose the size 48.

Now, I won't get into the depths of this line of reasoning at this point, but I thought it critical to at least present this explanation because our Evangelical friends are very caring and intelligent people. Whenever we as Catholics, Protestants, or Evangelicals come across theology which is outside our understanding (and beyond evident reason), we should at least take the time to figure out the underlying mote and rationale for that theology. Only from that type of sincere investigation can we come to love and respect our fellow Christian and hold with them a sincere debate.

3.3 Death Row

Once I accepted that Evangelicals follow a sincere thought process they believe reconciles Predestined Individual Election with human-will (though I did not agree with it), I was able to more carefully attend to various preachers as they explained TULIP.

The first thing I sought was a preacher, anywhere, who could explain the basic *fairness* within the Reformed theology. I thought, 'If Calvinists can't find a way to explain their core beliefs after nearly five hundred years of the Reformation, then maybe they need to seriously reconsider their doctrines.'

One of the leading Reformed theologians in America, who has lately passed away, used an analogy that assumed we are all Totally Depraved. Due to our depraved natures and inherent rebellion against God, we all deserve eternal damnation. We are like a group of men and women on death row, each convicted of murder. God, however, is like a governor who decides to pardon *some* of those justly condemned for death.

Is the governor's pardon of some, but not all, this pastor asked, unfair or unjust?

He argued that those who remain on death row do not receive any injustice, for they are being punished justly for their crimes. The governor has only exercised mercy for those he has pardoned. Similarly, the reprobate (those not chosen to receive saving grace) are simply doomed to hell as just punishment for their sins. There are therefore only two outcomes for the human person; either justice or mercy.

However, if we really consider this analogy in terms of the complete theology defined by TULIP, we must conclude that there is a group of men and women on death row condemned for crimes and sins the governor (God) gave them no chance, and no choice, but to commit.

And here is where we really get to the crux of the issue for Reformed theology.

If God was merely a bystander who zoomed by Earth one day and saw all these human beings destined for hell due to their sins and then decided to save a few, perhaps we could praise him for his grace and mercy. What is overlooked by TULIP, however, is that God is God. He is not merely a bystander.

If we are Totally Depraved due to the very nature of the souls we are born with, then he, as God, is the one and only power who created us that way. According to Calvinist theology, God created us and, following the Fall, he changed our natures so we are now *incapable* of *not* sinning. He took from us any chance to do or believe or act differently to avoid eternal damnation in hell. In punishment for a single sin of Adam, God punished each of us by eternally keeping us in enmity to him.

We can, I suppose, think of God as a computer programmer who sets the rules that any program which mistakenly provides the answer of '5' to the question, 'What is 2 + 2??' will be immediately deleted. But then God programs all of his subroutines to answer the question 'What is 2 + 2?' with the answer '5'.

Would God, the programmer, act 'fairly' to the programs he deleted for incorrectly answering this summation? Even if he decided that every tenth program that answers '5' will not be deleted, is he being fair when deleting of the other subroutines that could only provide that false answer?

If God created us Totally Depraved, or made us Totally

Depraved following the Fall of Adam and Eve, or 'programmed' the human race to automatically become Totally Depraved once Adam decided to eat the fruit of the tree, then the fact we are all on spiritual 'death row' in the first place is a terrible injustice. We are all from the beginning of our lives suffering injustice, for we have had no chance but to sin and completely turn away from God.

And for those who might argue that the doctrine of Total Depravity does not hold that God created us that way – who then is your God? Who then are 'the rulers...the authorities...the powers of this dark world and...the spiritual forces of evil in the heavenly realms' (Eph. 6:12) who bound up the power of God, stole his creation from him, and changed the souls of his human race?

Therefore, in our analogy, the 'elect' the 'governor' pardons are only getting a reprieve from the injustice they were also cursed with, while those left behind on death row continue to be unjustly punished for errors and crimes they have had no choice but to commit. Even in our flawed human existence, many governors go out of their way to look at death row cases with the intent of finding extenuating circumstances behind the crimes that were committed. Perhaps the criminal was forced to do the crime. Perhaps he or she was mentally unfit at the time of committing the crime to avoid their actions.

But, somehow, those following Reformed theology want us to believe our loving, merciful, and just God would not look upon us with similar compassion and allow for these same extenuating circumstances. Extenuating circumstances that he himself created, giving us no spiritual life within us, no real way to know right from wrong, no way to have the slightest desire to move even the first small step toward the good. By creating our souls as he has, we are forced to commit the crimes we commit. By making us Totally Depraved, we have been created mentally unfit to respond to God. All this because of the single sinful choice of another.

God, we are asked to believe, is like a social studies teacher who set up her class to be entirely graded upon a single final exam. If an individual student passes the test, they are given an 'A' for the class. If they fail, they are kicked out of class altogether with no hope of earning a passing grade.

The eager and somewhat nervous students show up to take the test to discover that the teacher has divided them into two groups. When the kids in the first group open their exams, they find the test booklets only have a space for their names, and their names are already neatly typed in the booklets. As they look around to each other in bewilderment, they realize there are some in their group who are good students, some who are poor students, some who participate in class, some who participate only with bad behavior and interruption. But, they realize, all of the kids in their group have blonde hair.

The rest of the class is moved to a second room and all the lights are turned off. These darker haired young men and women, this second group or good students and poor, participants and interrupters, open their tests to find all the questions written entirely in an ancient Babylonian text.

We are asked to believe this second group of students, when they fail their tests, have still been treated fairly by their teacher and only received the grades they deserved, for the teacher had every right to set up the test however she wanted. And the other group, those who didn't even have to fill in their names, well, we are told these students should in fact give praise, thanks and glory to the teacher for her kindness to them.

But is this *really* what Evangelicals believe and teach? Or am I, a Catholic possessing no graduate level theological teaching in the Reformed tradition, misrepresenting what Calvinists believe?

This question was answered during a radio question-and-answer session held by the same leading preacher whose analogy initially caused me pause. To paraphrase (only slightly), the pastor recounted:

Little Johnny from Florida asked the question, "Did God know that Adam and Eve would sin?"

The preacher chuckled and said, "Johnny, if this answer keeps you up tonight, then you have the makings of a theologian."

"The answer is," the pastor continued, "not only did he know it, he ordained it. He wills everything that

comes to pass in history. It was through his good pleasure that there was the Fall. He created for his own glory a world that would fall into sin."

But, this is merely an answer to a question asked at a conference. What is the 'official' Reformed teaching? We need go no further than to the Westminster Confession (1646):

By this (Adam's) sin they fell from their original righteousness and fellowship with God, and so became dead in sin and completely polluted in all their faculties and parts of body and soul. Since Adam and Eve are the root of all mankind, the guilt for this sin has been imputed to all human beings, who are their natural descendants and have inherited the same death in sin and the same corrupt nature. This original corruption completely disinclines, incapacitates, and turns us away from every good, while it completely inclines us to every evil. (Chapter 6, Paragraphs 2-4)

And why did God create we humans incapable of loving him in the slightest? Why, according to those of the Reformed faith, are most of us predestined individually for hell?

In order to manifest his glory, God has ordered that

some men and angels should be predestined to everlasting life and that others should be fore-ordained to everlasting death. (Westminster Confession, Chapter 3, Paragraph 3).

Think about that.

God, for his own glory, predestined people to everlasting death (in hell)? With no hope. No chance. No ability to grow out of the souls he created them with. No mercy from a savior who came specifically to save other specific human beings, and not them.

Logically, if we believe the Calvinists, God forced us to sin. They claim otherwise, but if God had a predestined plan that I personally would be condemned to hell, then there always *had* to be a me, and I always *had* to be created Totally Depraved, which therefore meant that Adam and Eve *had* to eat the forbidden fruit of the Tree. God forced me to be born, not with Adam's imperfect communion with him following the Fall, but under the absolutely sure curse of irresistible sin, ending up in torment for living in the only manner made possible for me.

This is an injustice. God, according the Calvinist doctrine, has therefore provided only two outcomes, mercy, or injustice. And how can that possibly be for his glory?

3.4 An Aside – The Fall

The Evangelical focus on the Fall, through a literal interpretation of the first chapters of Genesis, is critical for TULIP. Without the Fall, there is no Total Depravity. Without Total Depravity, there are no Five Points and the Calvinist theology of salvation breaks down irreparably.

Assuming for argument's sake that the story of Adam and Eve reflects two historical persons, there are three options available to us.

Option 1 –God made all human beings to be born, in Calvinist language, Totally Depraved, but God provided our first grandparents (Adam and Eve) a period of 'probation.' They shared an enhanced fellowship with God until they disobeyed, breaking their probation and leading God to toss them out of the Garden of Eden to live again within their natural, depraved states. This option poses to us at least two distinct and difficult questions. First, why would God create humanity Totally Depraved? Second, if Adam and Eve were naturally in a state where they had no desire to follow or love God at all, how did they ever behave properly in the Garden at all? Did God provide for them at that point an Irresistible Grace? If so, then why did God remove this Grace to enable them to Fall?

Option 2 – The second option adheres to the claim we read early in Genesis that after Creation, that God found everything 'good.' Adam and Eve, therefore, were created good, but then after they disobeyed God, God infused them (and us) with Total Depravity. The question here, of course, is *why*, if Adam and Eve were created 'good' and shared a direct fellowship with God, did they then fail? *How* could they fall? In other words, if Total Depravity means that there is *no* desire to be with God, then 'good' would imply a holiness in which they by nature would necessarily follow God entirely and the first humans would be protected (preserved) by that same God whose sovereign power cannot be overcome. More importantly for us, once Adam and Eve fell, why did God then condemn all their offspring eternally to be born Totally Depraved based upon this one bad choice? Why would a God who supposedly sent his Son to offer mercy to some in his creation for his own glory not have been glorified even more by forgiving Adam and Eve for their one sin and maintaining our souls with the good he created within the first pair or humans?

Option 3 – The third option is that we were all, including Adam and Eve, created 'good' but this 'goodness' through God's sovereign Will included human-will. This human-will provides the opportunity to accept or reject God and/or his commands. While Adam and Eve obeyed, they continued to live in direct fellowship with God in the Garden (as we will eventually live in direct fellowship with God in heaven). When they, however, chose to reject God, at least temporarily, they were forced from the Garden. None of their descendants could again enjoy the perfect communion with God, but we share the same basic goodness and the same human-will. In terms of their direct offspring, Abel chose to offer sacrifices to God that were acceptable. The other son, Cain, chose to reject God, sin, and was rejected. But in God's comments to Cain – even Cain – in Genesis 4 proves that even the first children of Adam and Eve were not born Totally Depraved, they had a choice.

If you do what is right, will you not be accepted? But if you do not do what is right, sin is crouching at your door; it desires to have you, but *you must rule over it.* (Gen. 4:7)

3.5 Evident Reason and Beyond

As I listened to sermon after sermon, I circled back to where I started. Back to the realization that Calvinist theology attempted to disprove the need of Catholic sacraments and practices and ended up painting a portrait of an unfair God. Unfair, that is, unless we are convinced through the scriptures, and beyond reasonable doubt, that this is the reality God has created.

If, as Luther said, through *evident reason* and scriptural proof we discover a God who is unfair in these ways, predestining some individually to eternal torment from the beginning of time, then it is we who need to change our definitions of fair and unfair. And yet, even if I can make the case through evident reason that the ideas outlined by TULIP are incorrect, I also need to demonstrate a reasonable option to TULIP in the biblical texts. Otherwise, we will continue to have one group of Christians attacking fellow Christ-followers as being not only unsaved but un-savable, outside their small group of those Predestined Individually for Election.

So, eventually, we need to turn our sights directly toward the same scriptures used to support PIE, not reading them blindly and without a guide, but reading them with Evangelical and Calvinist concepts in mind to point us to those specific chapters and verses in which some find proofs for the theologies contained in TULIP.

Therefore, let us look once more at the concept of Predestined Individual Election and see where the scriptures take us. And let us all start where it would naturally seem best, the point where most Evangelicals start – within Romans, by Paul.

3.6 Patience

Let's first take a moment to consider the consequences of what we might discover. I have lived in part within the Evangelical world for over a decade now, and many if not most Evangelicals are taught that since they are right, and all other Christ followers stand against their theology, the rest of us are not truly Christian in the first place. We have been predestined to continue as eternal enemies of God and we will one day pay the price for our very existence through condemnnation in hell.

What does it mean, however, if there is another more consistent and evidently true interpretation of the Bible that leads away from TULIP? Does that mean that Evangelicals are not Christ followers? That they can never be forgiven? That they are doomed to eternal torment simply for the glory of God?

No.

It is not condemnation of others we seek, nor believe in. We welcome our brethren and any sincere effort they make to better understand and obey the ways of God. Even if TULIP is proved to be completely in error, those who are brought up in this error and stand by what they believe serves the Lord will, we pray, not be held accountable for those beliefs as sins.

Chapter 4

The Structure of Romans

I listed to a review of the 1979 book from writer John Robinson entitled <u>Wrestling with Romans</u>. The book's title was appropriate because the reviewer said the writer's goal was the discovery of a systematic way to overcome the difficulty of reading PIE into the Book of Romans.

The book suggested that Paul wrote Romans as a long ramp, or set of maritime locks, which built upon itself throughout the first eight chapters of the book, leading toward the heights of the Apostle's theological theme, found in chapter 9. Paul's writing, accordingly, then descends as the remaining chapters trail off in importance and were used by Paul only to support his main thesis. In this interpretation, the author reflects many other Evangelical teachers and pastors I have studied who also profess Romans 9 as the very pinnacle of Christian theology and the key to the Bible. As the Evangelical preacher, John Piper, wrote:

There are two experiences in my life that make Romans 9 one of the most important chapters in shaping the way I think about everything, and the way I have been led in ministry.[4]

Interestingly, Pastor Piper follows up this comment with proof again of the previous claims in this book,

"When I entered seminary, I believed in the freedom of my will...."

One of the things that struck me about <u>Wrestling with Romans'</u> theme, however, is that we should always try to read Romans (or any of the New Testament texts) as it would have come into contact with its initial intended audience. We should not only search for what we think God is trying to teach us today, two thousand years later in a culture very, very different from first-century Rome, or Ephesus, or Jerusalem. We should also decipher the most probable issues the writers addressed when they wrote to very specific infant churches in the decades immediately following the Resurrection.

It appears most of the writing in the New Testament follows a pattern where the writer lays out his initial theme early in the text and then supports that thesis through subsequent portions of their book and letter. If nothing else, we should remember the difficulty in writing, copying, and relaying these ancient texts at the time, which made brevity an important consideration. Revelation is probably the one text furthest from this pattern in that it necessarily builds to a final crescendo when Jesus comes into his glory at the end of time. But even a not-so-careful reading of the rest the New Testament supports my theory.

Matthew quickly made the point to his largely Jewish readers of his Gospel that Jesus is the Jewish Messiah. We can make the case that even though there are powerful scenes in different parts of his Gospel, and extremely important moments like the Last Supper, everything he wrote after the initial chapter supports his initial assertion.

John even more clearly lays out his main theme that Jesus is the Word of God and divine in the opening verses of his Gospel. Thereafter can be seen many recollections of Jesus' life concerning the circumstances and teachings the apostle experienced first-hand, all of which explain John's initial claim.

Another technique we should consider is to read the books as the author would have read it. I, as the author of this book, will reread and edit starting from the beginning and work my way through the rest of the text. Knowing that I want to further divide the book into chapters would enable me, perhaps, to lay out multiple ideas at the beginning of various chapters and use the rest of each chapter to prove my points. But the chapter divisions we follow now in Holy Scripture were not used by the writers themselves; they were added for our convenience much later.

My point is that, as a writer, I strongly question the assertion that Paul waited to write his main theme of Romans until the ninth chapter of the book. Certainly, it sometimes takes a while to build the foundation of common understanding between the writer and reader before a theme makes sense, but I don't believe eight entire chapters opening this book are simply foundational. Plus, Paul's writing was sent to already founded local churches and current believers, men and women who already stood upon the apostolic foundations of the faith.

In a time when writers had limited ability and resources to write and transport letters, it was critical to get to their main point quickly. So maybe we need to look at Romans from the beginning to figure out what the overarching themes were within Paul's mind. Then we can figure out whether there is consistent theme maintained throughout the book, including Chapter 9.

Let us explore Romans 9 now with a careful ear toward the words Evangelicals use to support the idea that the idea of God's sovereignty always outweighs our interpretation of his justice and fairness. Let us judge if this really is what Paul preached? At the very least, let us discover if we can interpret Paul's words in any other consistent and logical way? In other words, are there perhaps two reasonable interpretations of this chapter of Romans? If there are, we should then look to the rest of Romans to determine which of these two concepts is better supported. Armed with this scriptural proof, we will then use Luther's idea of evident reason to help us conclude what the Holy Spirit is guiding us to understand regarding our individual paths toward heaven through the life, death, and resurrection of Christ.

For my Catholic readers, it may feel uncomfortable or unnecessary to pick apart, verse by verse, a single chapter of scripture to support or disprove certain points of theology. But, if the goal is to convince Evangelicals that an 'us vs. them' view of salvation is incorrect, this form of detailed investigation of the Bible is necessary. We need to understand the arguments made against non-Evangelical faiths from the text of this chapter. We must be armed with a clear explanation of what we really find in the Apostle's words before we are challenged.

4.1 Brothers in Arms

Form many, the final and highest step upon the peak of Reformed biblical theology is found roughly halfway through Romans 9. Paul reaches back to a very familiar story in the Old Testament about Jacob and Esau. For those who might be unfamiliar, Abraham's son Isaac had twin sons of his own. Esau was the older brother, and therefore the one through whom the Chosen People of Israel should have descended. But, through some questionable wheeling and dealing, the younger son Jacob received the blessing of his father and through his lineage then came the Jewish people.

Evangelicals believe they find strong support for their doctrines of predestination and election when Paul writes,

"Yet, before the twins were born or had done anything good or bad - in order that God's purpose in election might stand: not by works but by him who calls – she (the twins' mother Rebekah) was told, "The older will serve the younger." Just as it is written, "Jacob I loved, but Esau I hated" (Rom. 9:13).

Then (and this seems to be extremely persuasive to many Calvinists preachers I have heard speak on the subject) in verses 14 through 21, Paul points out that he understands there will be some who claim the choice of one brother over another in such a way may be considered unfair. The Apostle asks, "What then shall we say? Is God unjust?" He then quotes Exodus in the Old Testament to answer this charge, "I will have mercy on whom I have mercy and will have compassion on whom I have compassion" (Ex. 33:19).

In the minds of many Evangelical preachers I have heard or read, Paul's next reference makes this point even more forcibly, as he recalls the Old Testament story of God 'hardening' Pharaoh's heart, "I raised you up for this very purpose, that I might display my power in you" (Rom. 9:17).

Evangelicals believe Paul here knows what his reader's natural reaction will be when faced with the idea that God actively forces someone to resist his will, and Paul seems to preempt that concern as well. He writes, "One of you will say to me 'Then why does God still blame us? For who resists his will?'" (Rom. 9:19).

With no more context or reflection on these words, it is easy to see how they can be interpreted as many Evangelicals interpret them. As a one-time relatively untrained listener of the Word, I found myself experiencing many 'ah-ha' moments as I heard these Calvinist arguments for the first time. You can certainly make the case that Paul speaks here about God choosing one person individually and not choosing another person individually. You can even make the claim that Paul asserts even before we are born God not only can, but already has, determined our fates just as he decided the fates of the two Old Testament brothers individually, Jacob and Esau.

Once you accept these Evangelical interpretations as your foundational understanding of Romans, you can read find other parts of the New Testament, including other areas within Romans which employ the terms 'election' and 'chosen' and 'predestined,' to defend PIE. You can, logically, support the case that our salvation or damnation is entirely dependent upon God's sovereign will, has nothing to do with our own personal choices in terms of faith or 'works,' and has already been determined from all eternity past. I mention this because for us to trust one another, we need to reaffirm that neither side of this issue considers the other either stupid or insincere.

In the Protestant-oriented Life Application Bible (NIV version) I have read for many years, the subtitle of Romans 9 (verses 6-29) is 'God's Sovereign Choice' (note – subtitles are the editor's additions to the text, not part of the scriptures themselves). I think most Christians, whether Catholic,

Protestant or otherwise, would agree God is God and we are not, and God does have the sovereign right to choose what our fates are should he so desire.

But to maintain that God does do this for everyone personally and individually from all eternity, with no respect for our choices or faith in this life, well, this brings the issue far from mere theory and makes it very, very practical. Subsequently, this core Calvinist belief needs to be fully vetted. If Romans 9 is the linchpin, then a closer look at this chapter is imperative. A closer look at not only Paul's words, but also the reason why he wrote them will be of significant help.

4.2 Why did Paul Write?

I would like to introduce another, perhaps obvious, theme in Paul's writing throughout this chapter of Romans. This is certainly not my original idea; I've heard it mentioned even by Evangelical preachers to one extent or another, usually in an attempt to quickly dismiss the concept.

It is clear that the Jews at the time of Christ and Paul had a very passionate understanding that they alone were the Chosen People of God. They maintained a very strict separation between themselves and the Gentiles. Therefore, within the new Christian church, made up of former Jews and former Gentiles, Paul had to overcome the prejudices of his former Jewish family.

In fact, while the NIV uses the subtitle 'God's Sovereign

Choice' for the middle of Romans 9, the section preceding this is subtitled, 'Paul's Anguish Over Israel.' The subtitle for the section immediately following 'God's Sovereign Choice,' is 'Israel's Unbelief.' Even these insights from the Protestant editors of the NIV (New International Version) make it difficult to believe that between discussions about 'Israel,' the Apostle diverted his attention toward theology concerning our individual predestined fates.

Paul attacked his goals of breaking down prejudices and building bridges within the new Christian faith by reminding his Jewish readers, "for not all who were descended from Israel are Israel" (Rom. 9:6). He makes it plain that simple physical descendance within the nation of Israel does not bring one into the spiritual family, the spiritual Israel, of God. He continues,

> Nor because they are his descendants, are they all
> Abraham's children. On the contrary, "It is through
> Isaac that your offspring will be reckoned." In other
> words, it is not the children by physical descent who
> are God's children, but it is the children of the prom-
> ise who are regarded as Abraham's offspring, (Rom.
> 9:7-8).

By stating clearly that the offspring will be reckoned not through either 'Jacob' or 'Esau' but through their father, Isaac, Paul begins to lay the case that both the Gentile offspring of

Esau and the Jewish offspring of Jacob can now enter equally into the new spiritual family of Christ.

Paul acknowledges the reality within the infant local churches of his time and used 'Jacob' to represent the Jewish nation (the elect of the Old Testament) and 'Esau' to represent the Gentile nations. He emphasized the past separation between the Jew and the Gentile in Old Testament times in the verse we mentioned earlier, "Jacob I loved and Esau I hated" (Rom. 9:13).

It was this exact verse, in fact, which brought me to consider whether there is another theme to this chapter that better reflects the overarching concept Paul pressed home throughout Romans. Was there another explanation for these words more closely associated with the proper Christian doctrines of God's fairness and righteousness? Is there another logical path found within these sentences that leads us away from a divisive Calvinist interpretation, or are we left with only the possibility of Predestined Individual Election on a human-wide scale?

Did Paul really mean God 'hated' Esau personally from the beginning of time, and that God 'loved' Jacob simply due to his sovereign choice before either twin was even born? If he did, does that mean we can expand this understanding universally to all human beings, clinging to the doctrine that some few of us were eternally chosen to be God's friends while all others were doomed before they did or thought anything to be his enemies?

Note: 'Jacob' was used throughout the Old Testament as a replacement for the people of Israel. An abbreviated list of such instances is found at the end of this book.

4.3 Esau

The first thing I did was to look at the reference cited in my NIV Bible. When Paul writes that God loved Jacob, he quoted from the book of Malachi. Malachi is the last of the Old Testament prophets, his book coming just before Matthew opens the New Testament era.

As the oracle of Malachi begins, he confirms that he is giving a 'Word of the Lord to Israel'. And what is God telling Israel?

"I have loved you", says the Lord. "But you ask, 'How have you loved us?' (Mal. 1:2)

Malachi then mentions Esau and Jacob.

Was not Esau Jacob's brother?" the Lord says. "Yet I have loved Jacob, but Esau I have hated, and I have turned his mountains into a wasteland and left *his inheritance* to the desert jackals. (Mal. 1:3).

God offers through Malachi the idea that Israel, his

Chosen People of the Old Testament period, has indeed been specially loved and blessed, using 'Jacob' as substitute name for the entire nation. He is clearly not referring to Jacob as an individual, for he is answering the direct question from Jacob's descendants who have asked God to prove how he has loved *them.*

In the same way, he clearly does not write about 'Esau' in terms of Esau the individual man. Malachi uses 'Esau' in verse 3 as a substitute name for those Gentile nations God did not specially bless ('love') with his commandments and protections. The Gentiles are referred to here as Esau's *inheritance,* and just as God answered how he loved the Jews who were contemporaries with Malachi, so he also speaks in his chapter about the contemporary descendants of Esau.

Paul, deeply versed in the Old Testament, clearly knew his readers would understand the reference. So, it makes sense that in writing Romans 9 (and especially this key verse used by Evangelicals to hold together the concepts of *individual* predestined election), the Apostle almost certainly used 'Jacob' and 'Esau' in the same way Malachi used them in his prophecy. Paul, like Malachi, seems to use Jacob to represent the New Testament followers of Christ, as the 'nation' making up of a new Chosen People. Those who have joined this group and given themselves to Jesus, this new nation, are those who God 'loves'. Those who have not believed in Christ (Jew or Gentile) are now placed in the camp of the New Testament nation of Esau. The group of humans who God now 'hates.'

Now, if Paul is talking about Esau and Jacob as a reflection of us being personally predestined for election by God or personally and eternally predestined for damnation, he would not have chosen to quote Malachi, who clearly used the same names to speak not about individuals but about two groups of people. Throughout the Old Testament, which Paul would have known in great detail, there are dozens of times when the writers use 'Jacob' in place of 'Israel' (the people).

Had Paul (or Malachi) wanted to display God's eternal choice about Jacob and Esau simply as individuals, he would have simply laid out the case from Genesis that God, despite the cultural norms of the time, chose Jacob – the younger twin – to pour out untold love and affection and blessings upon. He would have demonstrated that this godly 'love' and apparent blessings toward Jacob individually also included his personal eternally salvation while Esau's earthly punishments proved his spiritual fate was among the eternally lost.

Instead, Malachi writes about the *people* Israel, and speaks about the '*inheritance* of Esau' (the people or offspring) instead of Esau the man. Malachi does not seem to be teaching the Jews of his time (the 'us' written about in Mal. 1:2) anything regarding individual salvation at all, but instead answered the Jewish challenges of his time regarding God's relationship with their nation.

4.4 Hated?

If Romans 9 used Esau to reflect eternally decreed hatred for the older brother, then we should see at least some reflection of this in the book of Genesis. Esau, of course, was not a perfect person, far from it. But we certainly cannot point to Jacob and claim the younger brother was chosen by God from before birth to be especially righteous. Jacob, in fact, outright stole his brother's inheritance by deceiving his aged, nearly blind, father.

As he did, following the adultery and murder committed by King David, God can forgive any sin. But to claim that Jacob was marked from birth to live a faithful and righteous life while Esau was destined to live a wholly evil life simply cannot be proven by scripture. Considering the two men with regards to the emphasis in the New Testament toward 'faith' and 'repentance,' we cannot claim Jacob was specially endowed in these areas, particularly when compared to his older brother.

The facts we read in the Old Testament are quite the opposite. In a little discussed section of Genesis, at the start of Chapter 28, Isaac and his wife Rebekah send Jacob away to protect him from Esau's anger. Jacob is commanded not to marry foreign women. In verses 8 and 9, Esau recognizes God's command and obeys in the only way he could, marrying a woman from within his own people as Jacob had been ordered. In this respect, at least, Esau sought to obey the Lord.

Even more startling, when we continue to read the story of Esau and Jacob from this episode forward, not only is there no reference implying personal damnation for one son versus the other, but in terms of their personal lives from an earthly standpoint, we must come away with the idea that God specifically blessed Esau. Even though Jesus makes it clear that financial blessings, or lack thereof, do not necessarily reflect God's blessing or curse, the record we read in Genesis points clearly to God's love for Esau as an individual.

By the time we arrive at Genesis 33, we are shown Jacob coming back to Esau after having done his older brother great harm. Jacob is in a state of fear and trembles before his brother, begging for forgiveness. While wealthy in his own right, Jacob's family and possessions are far overshadowed by the enormous blessings his older brother enjoys. But more importantly than their financial wealth, can we decipher anything from the Old Testament account that points toward the internal, spiritual makeup of the two men?

We are shown this in Genesis 33:4. Despite his younger brother's deceit against him, "Esau ran to Jacob and embraced him; threw his arms around his neck and kissed him."

In other words, it is Esau who fulfilled Jesus's later command to forgive one's brother. Esau certainly does not seem from this Biblical account to have been spiritually doomed, or 'hated', for all eternity. He is shown to us to be materially wealthy, and even if he did not have a perfect soul, he at least possessed a loving and forgiving one (far from Totally Depraved).

Even in the New Testament, we read of God's blessing upon Esau:

> (God) By faith Isaac blessed Jacob and Esau in regard
> to their future. (Heb. 11:20)

4.5 A Clear Purpose

Paul likely would have been driven to address conflicts between the Jewish and Gentile converts to the new Christian faith. Gentiles entering the church would naturally entertain many questions concerning how and why God would have denied their ancestors for over a thousand years while communing closely with the Jews. Jewish Christians – after their people's obedience and sacrifices to God for centuries – would have wondered if all this effort was in vain, for now even the despised Gentiles were being accepted through Christ.

In Romans 9, then, we find Paul first defending God's decision to choose the Jewish race as a people to be specially blessed during the Old Testament period instead of the Gentile nations. He used the names of Jacob and Esau to represent these two communities. We might therefore not find a description in this chapter of Predestined Individual Election at all, but instead a description of the election of one new group of believers (Christians) as being 'loved' as 'Jacob' (the Jews) was once 'loved,' and another group (unbelievers in Christ) being 'hated' as 'Esau' (the Gentiles) once was.

The choice of which group each of his readers belonged to was no longer due to their lineage, but now at least partially determined by their choices to trust in, and obey, Jesus.

Paul began Romans 9 confirming his wish that the Israelites of his day might still be saved. But not all Jews came to faith in Christ, therefore the idea that the Jews as a collective group remained God's Chosen People was proven false by the Apostle's real-life experience. Only those now expressing and living within the Christian faith, regardless of their background, enjoyed the hope of salvation. If Paul used Jacob in this chapter to represent the Jewish nation, then he wrote, essentially, that there were those who still shared in the benefits of that *elect* Jewish nation through their communion within the Body of Christ.

Paul's angst at the time he wrote his letter to Rome was that the majority of this 'elect' Jewish race to which he physically belonged had not accepted Christ as their savior. Paul did not see these Jews as being *predestined* individually for eternal damnation. He clearly did not believe that God predestined every human within the Jewish nation to be automatically and individually saved from all eternity past in a spiritual sense. But neither, as we will see when we discuss Romans 11, did the Apostle believe those who currently disbelieved Christ were eternally chosen for that doom by the Father.

Piecing the words of Paul together opens before us the awareness of two logical interpretations of Romans 9. The first, which I've considered thus far to be the Calvinistic or Evangelical outlook, is that Paul wrote about God picking individuals for salvation or damnation (Jacob personally over his brother Esau personally) from the very beginning of time using nothing but his sovereign will as his guide. The other possible interpretation is that Paul wrote to his two groups of readers, former Jews and former Gentiles, who were making decisions to join him in following Christ, and thus working their way toward heaven, or deny the Savior. He tried to answer the very difficult questions that must have troubled the early Church as former enemies came together within the single earthly body of Jesus.

The core question for today's Christian, of course, is which of these two interpretations is more correct. It may very well be the case that both interpretations are so evidently *possible* that those on the either side of this argument should see those supporting the other side as being sincere Christians. Perhaps we can also pull back a bit to see the bigger picture, acknowledging that there are positive factors in both interpretations. For example, if you currently favor the idea of that Jacob and Esau reflect Predestined Individual Election, perhaps the possibility that Romans 9 instead teaching that Paul used Jacob and Esau to represent *communities* of believers will help motivate deeper engagement with the broader church community instead of only focusing upon one's personal relationship with Christ. If you favor reading Romans Chapter 9 as Paul using Jacob and Esau as explaining how God established the Old Testament plan for two 'nations,' then perhaps you can gain comfort believing that once you decide to toss your hat in with the saved community, you should still maintain deep humility and reliance upon God's grace, as is common within the Calvinist community.

4.6 The Guide of History

Should we focus more on what the biblical writers meant to say to their audiences, or should we assume God's words were equally 'for us' today, interpreted into our own time, culture and circumstances? The process we use to interpret our own historical knowledge should make it obvious that we must never forget that the individual books of the Bible were written in a specific time by a specific person to a specific group with a specific goal in mind. Consider the case of Abraham Lincoln. He wrote many reconciling words to placate Southerners before the Civil War, attempting to avoid armed conflict and maintain the union. We would not now take those words as meaning that Lincoln supported slavery. He had a different purpose for those messages altogether from the statements he made once engaged in an armed conflict.

That is not to say that the Bible is not a unique source. For we believe that it was inspired by God, who is timeless, to instruct us in his ways, which are timeless. If we go too far into pigeonholing the scriptures into singular times and places, we will fall into traps such as the one some Evangelicals fall into when they claim, for example, that the Gospel accounts (especially Matthew) were only written for the Jews and therefore have little relevance for modern Christians.

So, let's again consider the challenges Paul must have faced not only in Rome but in most of the first generation of Christian churches. Certain converts came to Christianity from Jewish roots and others came from Gentile backgrounds. Less than a decade or two earlier, these two groups of people would not talk or live or even be in the presence of the other. The Jewish side previously considered Gentiles unclean. Those outside the Jewish ranks certainly felt the Chosen People of the Old Testament were, at the very least, snobby.

Paul's task as he spread this revolutionary new Christian faith and supported the infant local churches was to establish and maintain unity between these two groups. To do so, he had to explain God's plan and purpose throughout the Old Testament era in a manner both sides would understand.

What was God's plan with the Jewish nation leading to the coming of Christ? And now, after his resurrection, why were both Jews and Gentiles being called equally to a new state of faith and grace? Paul had to convince his fellow Jews that God equally loved and accepted the Gentiles and they could, through Christ, attain salvation. To the Gentiles, Paul had to convince them that they should want to be saved by a God who seemingly shunned them and their ancestors for the previous thousand years and more.

Paul had to explain to the Jews who had suffered so much in order to remain pure in their faith in God, the Jews who had spent so much time and effort adhering to a set of laws that were clearly uncomfortable at best, that all of a sudden the Gentiles - who lacked this background of suffering and self-denial - were in a position to receive the complete saving grace of God through Christ. For the non-Jews, Paul assured them when they heard their fellow Christians of a Jewish background tell them they still had to follow all of the tasks prescribed by the Old Testament law, they instead only had to rely upon their belief in Christ, joining his new church body and obeying the Lord.

We find models to help visualize Paul's work throughout history. Following the Revolutionary War, the new American government struggled to graft together the Patriots who defeated the British with those newly minted Americans who had supported the Crown during the war. The Bolsheviks in Russia strived to rebuild unity in the new Motherland full of new comrades, some of whom had been the peasants of the Old Russia, and some their aristocratic leaders. We humans face this type of situation often enough and sometimes, we make the transition work smoothly. At other times, old divisions and prejudices linger, damaging the spirit of whatever group or family survives.

Paul faced a divide between his Jewish and Gentile readers which was one of the oldest and deepest humanity has ever faced. The Jewish side considered the divide as a command from God himself. Overcoming this divide must have been a primary reason for his letter to the Romans. Unity was critical to bring Christ successfully into the first century world.

When we consider the context of Paul's references to the story of Jacob and Esau in Genesis, we must understand that Paul, as a leading Jewish scholar, knew the entire Old Testament in great detail. In that text, God often inspired his writers to address the human weakness that wells up in the form of jealousy. Jealousy justified as an argument against apparent unfairness. Paul knew well, for example, the words of the prophet Ezekiel:

Yet your people say, 'The way of the Lord is not just.'
But it is their way that is not just. If a righteous
person turns from their righteousness and does
evil, they will die for it. And if a wicked person turns
away from their wickedness and does what is just and
right, they will live by doing so. Yet you Israelites say,
'The way of the Lord is not just.' But I will judge each
of you according to your own ways. (Ez. 33:17-20)

But what was this statement in Ezekiel referring to? What led God's people to make the claim that, 'The way of the Lord is not just?' We find the answer in the same chapter:

> Therefore, son of man, say to your people, 'If some-
> one who is righteous disobeys, that person's former
> righteousness will count for nothing. And if someone
> who is wicked repents, that person's former wicked-
> ness will not bring condemnation. The righteous
> person who sins will not be allowed to live even
> though they were formerly righteous.' If I tell a
> righteous person that they will surely live, but then
> they trust in their righteousness and do evil, none of
> the righteous things that person has done will be
> remembered; they will die for the evil they have done.
> And if I say to a wicked person, 'You will surely die,'
> but they then turn away from their sin and do what
> is just and right— if they give back what they took in
> pledge for a loan, return what they have stolen,
> follow the decrees that give life, and do no evil—that
> person will surely live; they will not die. Ez. 33:12-16

In this case, we can find a direct correlation perhaps of
Old Testament Jews and New Testament converts protesting
a seemingly strange reality. The Old Testament 'elect' protested to Ezekiel that they had done well and were righteous
and that it was unfair for God to now forget their former
righteousness and punish them for their sins. In Paul's time,
he probably heard the same concerns. The Christians who

had previously been his fellow Jews most certainly complained – 'We and our people have served God for centuries and you are saying all that work is no good to us now? You are saying that there are Jews whose righteousness is now forgotten because they do not believe in Christ as we do?'

Likewise, the sinful people God forgave and accepted in Ezekiel were like the Gentiles Paul now addressed in Romans. The Apostle told those Gentiles who came from a culture of unbelief that they could still achieve righteousness through faith in Christ and their new righteousness would be remembered while their past crimes were now forgiven.

If Paul remembered these words of Ezekiel, as we must assume he did, he must have also understood their clear meaning. These words from God in the Old Testament clearly implied that just as the evildoers could decide to change their lives for good and be accepted by God, the elect could turn their backs to the Lord and then be counted among the fallen. Their salvation was not once for all, but hope remained ever present for each individual.

4.7 If, Then

At the risk of interrupting the flow of our discussion, it is beneficial to pause at this point. In the quotation from Ezekiel, we read the small yet thunderous word, 'if', as in "*if* someone righteous disobeys."

When I began attending Evangelical services, I did not yet

realize that Calvinist theology used a competing definition for this very small word, 'if.' Once I understood how this teeny-tiny two-letter word was used, however, I understood the rationale behind their Reformed interpretations of our salvation. Perhaps by stating this issue here, we can avoid much of the confusion I struggled with and enjoy a more lucid discussion concerning Romans and the rest of the New Testament.

It is amazing to me, as an electrical engineer growing up in a computer-based society, that theological truths can now be clearly explained in ways that were inaccessible to generations past. Any present-day computer programmer recognizes and understands the critical importance of the universal 'If...then' statement. This concept sits at the core of any computer code and represents fundamental decision points.

If X happens (the condition X is 'true'), *then* outcome Y must then occur. *If* X does not happen (the condition X is 'false'), *then* we always receive outcome Z. For example, a computerized thermostat in a home might be programmed to turn on the air conditioning if the room temperature goes above 75 degrees (24 degrees Celsius). A normal 'if/then' statement is programmed to read '*if* X (room temperature) is above 75 degrees, *then* do Y (turn on the air conditioner). *If* X is below 75 degrees, *then* do Z (turn off the air conditioner).

In a similar way, we find several 'If...then' statements in the Bible from Paul, from Our Lord, and from the other writers. "*If* you believe, you will have eternal life,' '*if* you do the will of God, you will become righteous,' and so forth.

The main issue then concerning Evangelical thought comes down to this: is the 'if' a *choice* we need to make, or is it a *status* we simply find ourselves living in?

For example, let's say I make the statement, 'If you move to Chicago, you will be cold all winter."

When I say this, the obvious interpretation is that you have a choice. The 'if' implies that you can make the decision to move to Chicago, or not to move to Chicago. If you move to Chicago, you will experience cold weather in the winter. If you chose not to move there, you will experience the weather your current locale.

However, reformed theology reads this backwards. It essentially rejects human-will, denying that the 'if' indicates a choice. Reformed theology, when reading the 'if/then' statements in the Bible, take these statements as simply expressing the outcome that is predestined to happen for those who find themselves already in one state of being or another. In other words, '*if* I find myself living in Chicago, *then* I will be cold all winter long.'

In other words, I normally would make statements such as these –

- *If* I choose to drive at twice the speed limit, *then* I will receive a ticket.
- *If* I choose to cheat on my taxes, *then* I will be fined.

- *If* I choose to faithfully study a foreign language, *then* I will learn to speak it.

So, too, when Christians read, 'obey or you will not inherit the Kingdom of God' (to paraphrase 1 Cor. 6:9), the obvious assumption is that this statement reflects a choice. God gave us his command to obey and *if* we make the wrong choice *then* we will not receive our reward.

The Evangelical interpretation of 'if, then' leads us to something like this.

- *If* I find myself behind the wheel of a car that is going far too fast, *then* I will receive a ticket.
- *If* my taxes have been filled out by someone incorrectly, *then* I will be fined.
- *If* I find that I've studied Spanish two hours a night, *then* hablo español.

In other words, when it comes to faith, when it comes to living out our Christian lives, we either assume that the scriptural *ifs* are *choices* and in making our choices we have some level of responsibility for the *thens* (outcomes). Or, we believe that our state in life is predetermined for us. We already find ourselves living in one *if* (reality), and so we simply live out the *then* already laid in place by the creator of the if. 'If,' for example, we find ourselves believing in Jesus solely due to God's intrusion in our lives and through his forced grace, *then* we will be saved.

This is a very important distinction which we have to get right to properly interpret such seemingly simple scriptural text such as –

> For whoever does the will of my heavenly Father is
> my brother (Mat. 12:50)

Jesus' words seem clear here. The first part of his statement is the 'if.' For the 'whoever' is a person with a choice to either do the Father's will, or not do the Father's will. Jesus then explains the 'then' for those who choose wisely – that person will now be Jesus' brother.

Reformed theology flips this inside out. The assumption is that through predetermined regeneration, the 'whoever' already is Jesus' brother and therefore has no choice but to experience the *then* in their lives, they will irresistibly do the Father's will.

'If's' are most often identified in scripture by calls for action, for the scriptures are motivating us to make the correct choices and do the right things. Paul uses these calls for action quite often in the book of Romans. We will cover many of these comments as we move through the book, but let's simply look as a few here to end our chapter:

> *If* you declare with your mouth, "Jesus is
> Lord," and believe in your heart that God raised him

from the dead, (*then*) you will be saved (Rom. 10:9, 'then' added).

And *if* they do not persist in unbelief, (*then*) they will be grafted in, for God is able to graft them in again (Rom. 11:23, 'then' added).

(*If you*) Do not conform to the pattern of this world, but be transformed by the renewing of your mind. *Then* you will be able to test and approve what God's will is—his good, pleasing and perfect will (Rom. 12:2, 'if you' added).

Chapter 5

From the beginning

We began our discussion in Romans 9 because that is where the idea of what we've summarized in this book as Predestined Individual Election (PIE) is, according to many Evangelicals pastors, most clearly demonstrated.

While God's irresistible, predestined choice for some of us to be individually elected for salvation (or damnation) may be one reasonable interpretation of this chapter, we already considered the probability that Romans 9 should be read differently. Instead of using Esau and Jacob to explain away the seeming unfairness of PIE, Paul's primary concern seemed to be the unification of Jew and Gentile under the new umbrella of Christianity. Romans 9, and the use of the Old Testament twins, were his attempt to answer some of the vexing questions that must have haunted the faith in the decades following the Resurrection as Jewish and Gentile converts found difficulties accepting one another.

The concept of PIE does not dive into the how and why of the elect's individual predestined election; that was covered in our initial discussion concerning the 'Doctrines of Grace'

(TULIP). PIE merely focuses upon the main definitions behind the Calvinist 'gospel,' that God predestines some individuals (and no others) for election to salvation, with no role or responsibility from the elect, and no hope for the reprobate.

Before we get into the later chapters of Romans and whether they also support this theory, we should begin 'from the beginning,' with the point in the first chapter of Romans which Evangelicals also believe they find proof that their doctrines are true. But before we get to Paul's opening paragraphs, let's look at chapters 2-7 to give ourselves plenty of context from which we can decipher God's truth.

TULIP maintains that we are all born Totally Depraved, but God chooses a few people individually to provide the grace of spiritual regeneration through the Holy Spirit. This regeneration turns once Totally Depraved souls into souls which believe in the saving power of Jesus. This faith in Jesus cannot be a result of anything we human beings do or say or think or feel; otherwise, the choice of accepting salvation through faith in Christ will at least in some part be due to our own efforts and choices and not entirely up to the sovereign will of God. Evangelical doctrines hold that we are spiritually dead and therefore incapable of cooperating with God's call in even the slightest way.

Now, to support their idea of Total Depravity specifically, Evangelicals point to Romans Chapter 3, verses 9 through 18. In this section, Paul quotes from the 14th and 53rd Psalms, and his words are used by nearly every Calvinist preacher I have heard as proof of our completely fallen natures.

> There is no one righteous, not even one, there is no one who understands, no one who seeks God. All have turned away, they have become altogether worthless; there is no one who does good, not even one. (Rom. 3:11-12 and Ps. 14:1-3 and Ps. 53: 1-3)

Now, taken by itself, we can certainly read this text as supportive of the concept of Total Depravity. If there is no one righteous and no one who seeks God, then anyone who is saved and who has faith must have it because God in his sovereignty chose that person individually to have faith.

But let us not forget that the Psalms Paul quoted were songs and, like any other song, they often dramatize, over-emphasize, and use poetic license. The object of a modern song-writer's love is never just a pretty girl, but the *'loveliest of all time.'* Another singer's angst over life is not simply a period of trouble, but the *'end of the world.'* Is it surprising then that the psalmist doesn't simply decry the sins he finds committed by the people around him but instead exclaims that *'there is no one who does good, not even one'*?

What's more important, however, is what Paul says in the verse he wrote before his quotation of this psalm. In Romans 3:9, Paul writes, "What shall we conclude then? Are we any better? Not at all! We have already made the charge the Jews and Gentiles alike are all under sin."

So, if one reads Romans 3 by itself (and not after jumping back from Chapter 9 with a particular theology already implanted in one's mind), we recognize that Paul is simply telling his fellow Jews, who thought they are spiritually better than the Gentiles, that they in fact were no better. He told the Jews who believed they were the elect that they, now living within a faith community which included ex-Gentiles, were no better off than their new brethren. He writes that even though he himself and his fellow Jews had the Old Testament laws by which they believed themselves superior to the Gentiles, that Law on its own could not save them. If Jews were already convinced that no Gentile 'was good, no not one,' then Paul uses the psalmist's words here to emphasize that this lack of righteousness is universal and includes them – the ex-Jews – as well.

One major problem that seemed to vex Paul at this time was the air of superiority maintained by the new Jewish Christians over the new Gentile Christians. The Jews considered themselves more important to God, still part of what their culture taught them was God's blessed elect. We know this by reading elsewhere in the New Testament (especially in the first chapter of Galatians) stories about the Jewish Christians demanding that the new Gentile Christians follow the old Jewish customs.

Read again what Paul writes to them prior to quoting the Psalms in Romans 3:

Now you, if you call yourself a Jew; if you rely on the law and brag about your relationship to God.... Circumcision has value if you observe the law, but if you break the law, you have become as though you had not been circumcised. If those who are not circumcised keep the law's commandments, will they not be regarded as though they were circumcised? (Rom. 2:17, 25-26)

The Jews who entered the new Christian Church, Paul wrote, were no better or worse than the one-time Gentiles due to their physical circumcision and membership within the Jewish nation. To reinforce this point, he recited the Old Testament Psalm his Jewish readers would have been well acquainted with. His theme in Chapter 3 does not seem to be that we are all entirely corrupt and spiritually dead as much as to say that in Christ's church there is no difference between Jew and Gentile, no benefit of simply having been brought up with the Old Testament faith. Whether Jew or Gentile, we all shared the trait that 'there is not one who does good.'

In the very next section (Rom. 3: 22-23), Paul further asserts this when he reminds his Jewish readers, "This righteousness from God comes through faith in Jesus Christ to all who believe. There is no difference, for all have sinned and fall short of the glory of God."

And, even more directly, in Romans 3:29, the Apostle states emphatically: "Is God the God of Jews only? Is he not the God of Gentiles too?"

As we attempt to discern Paul's meaning (is Romans 3 about individual predestination or a call for unity in the infant church?) we look not only at the context of Scripture but also the challenges the Church community faced at the time. We possess other writings from the same era showing that other church leaders shared in the Paul's effort to correct the Jewish converts who pressed the idea that the Old Testament Law was still required. Ignatius, the bishop of Antioch at the turn of the first century and probably taught by John the Apostle himself, wrote to the faithful as he neared martyrdom:

> Be not deceived with strange doctrines, nor with old fables, which are unprofitable. For if we still live according to the Jewish law, we acknowledge that we have not received grace.

Again, I am not here to claim there is no justification for the Calvinist interpretation. I am only suggesting at the very least there are two interpretations in Romans 3 which make sense. Those who hold either of these two interpretations should never treat other Christians as separated from Christ and less than our brothers and sisters simply because they believe differently in this area of the faith.

Now, I must admit, my Evangelical education concerning their process of Biblical study has helped me in many ways. I have listened to many pastors link a New Testament writer to something written in the Old Testament; their investigations do not end with the New Testament verse(s) alone. They often look at the text surrounding each citation to discover how the context of the Old Testament reference positions and explains the text.

In the same way, it is beneficial to look at the Psalm quoted by Paul in Romans 3. Since Paul's reference is understood by some as a powerful proof of TULIP, what is its true context within the Psalms themselves?

Paul's statement, "there is no one who does good, not even one," comes from Psalms 14:3. If no one does good, if not one person does the things of God, then shouldn't we assume Total Depravity?

Well, in the very next psalm, Psalm 15, David writes:

Lord, who may dwell in your sanctuary? Who may live on your holy hill? (Ps. 15:1)

His next words are interesting indeed:

He whose walk is blameless and who does what is righteous. (Ps. 15:2)

If Psalm 14 is interpreted to insist we are *all* Totally Depraved and incapable of doing, or even wanting to do good, what are we to conclude from the very next psalm which insists that there are those who are 'blameless,' and there are men and women who will do what is 'righteous'?

In the previous chapter in Romans, Paul quotes other Psalms. What themes does he promote through those citations? If we go for example, to Romans 2:6-8, Paul says that God "will give each person according to what he has done." This is quoted from Psalm 62:12. Paul continues, "To those who *by persistence* in doing good seek glory and honor and immortality, he will give eternal life. But for those who are *self-seeking* and who reject the truth and follow evil, there will be wrath and anger (Rom. 2:7-8).

Clearly, Paul instructs his readers here that they are capable of seeking good (and 'persisting' in this effort), and also capable of rejecting the truth. What's more, Paul clearly taught that what is important is not just our faith but also how that faith is expressed through our actions and works.

> For it is not those who *hear* the law who are righteous
> in God's sight, but it is *those who obey* the law who
> will be declared righteous. (Rom. 2:13)

Paul concludes the theme of this section of Romans by again speaking against any self-inflicted divide between his Jewish and Gentile brethren. He says both groups will receive either reward or punishment for their actions. He summarizes this by writing,

> There will be trouble and distress for every human
> being who does evil: first for the Jew, then for the
> Gentile; but glory, honor and peace for everyone who
> does good: first for the Jew, then for the Gentile. For
> God does not show favoritism. (Rom. 2:9-11)

He reiterates this point again, "All who sin apart from the law (referring to the Gentiles) will also perish apart from the law, and all who sin under the law (referring to the Jews) will be judged by the law" (Rom. 2:12).

So, as we see here in Romans 2 and 3, the saint established the theme that Christian Jews and Christian Gentiles should not quarrel about perceived differences and past wrongs. Gentiles and Jews both felt some level of unfairness in terms of how God treated them prior to the coming of Jesus Christ, and Paul carefully answers those questions and concerns. He lays out another belief, not just in the saving faith of Christians in Christ's redeeming work on the cross, but also the importance of the decisions we make and the works we do.

5.1 Romans 4

More than one Evangelical preacher has quoted the third verse from Romans 4, believing it confirmed TULIP. Paul wrote, "Abraham believed God and it was credited to him as righteousness" (Rom. 4:3). He followed this by stating, "to a man who does not work but trusts God who justifies the wicked, his faith is credited as righteousness" (Rom. 4:5).

Those who follow Calvinist theology point us to these verses and ask, "Isn't it clear then that we are saved by faith alone, and not through works?"

If we consider these two verses in light of the "If/Then" options we previously discussed, then perhaps there are individuals who suddenly find themselves in the state of having faith, and thus in a state of God-given salvation. The faith God forced upon them individually is something he then credits to them as righteousness, forgiving their sins and electing them to everlasting life.

On the other hand, if righteousness is garnered even the slightest bit through our actions and works (as Romans 2 explained to us), then our relationship with God is at least partially the result of our choices. And if we can make the righteous choices, we can certainly fall into unrighteous sins. If our choices have anything to do with our eventual fates, the five building blocks of TULIP fall in upon themselves one-by-one.

If we are called to make a choice, then our souls cannot have been made totally depraved. If our choice affects the outcome of the grace we are given, then that grace is not strictly unconditional. If God's commandments, which leave us 'no excuse' but to follow him, are given to all (represented by Jews and Gentiles in the scriptures), then Jesus' atonement on the Cross is not limited by God's predestined choice, but only due to our failures to live in faith and obedience. If a person at one point in their lives believes in Christ as Lord and Savior and later makes the wrong choices and suffers the loss of the Kingdom of God (see Ephesians 5 and Galatians 5), then the doctrines of irresistible grace and the perseverance of the saints must be in error.

Of course, all Christians acknowledge the critical impor-tance of our faith and that this faith is required for the for-giveness of sins. As a Catholic listening to Evangelical sermons, I want to say time and again, 'We Catholics believe in Christ. We believe we are saved through him. We don't think we can just give money to the Church or say ten Hail Mary's and somehow oblige God to welcome us into heaven even if we have no faith in Jesus.'

Our Church turned aside the Palegians who taught we can be perfect through our own power alone. We turned aside the semi-Palegians who claimed we have no need for grace at the beginning of our spiritual walk with God. But the body of Christ has never agreed in *anti-Pelagianism* in which there is a moment in life beyond which we need not obey God nor bear any responsibility for our ongoing sins!

Getting back to Romans 4, we first need to accept that there is a difference between 'works' and 'tasks.' The common perception concerning many of the Jewish leaders in Christ's day was that if they accomplished the prescribed religious tasks each day, those actions alone would bring them closer to God. Instead, Jesus saved some of his most scathing remarks for these 'hypocrites' who did the tasks but ignored the good 'works' of charity and love for God and their fellow man. What parent doesn't get angry with their child when, even though he or she complete all their chores each day, they sit in moody silence at the dinner table, refusing to interact with the family? What parent would not care more for their child helping a sibling than taking out the trash?

But God, the God the Jews followed – who *is* Jesus, his Father and the Holy Spirit - was and is the same God who gave the Jewish people not only the Ten Commandments but all of the rules and regulations we read about in the Old Testament. Done correctly, these 'works' and 'tasks' built a tightly knit Jewish nation and prepared the people for the coming of the Messiah.

Just as, for example, today's Bible studies are intended to do.

Just as, for example, the sacramental system is intended to do.

That said, beyond the two verses we mentioned above, I rarely hear much about the rest of Romans 4. In this chapter, Paul moved right back to his main theme – unity within the Christian faith for both the Jew and the Gentile. But where comes this unity? For Jews – they needed to accept that the old Law by itself, without Christ, would no longer save them. For Gentiles, they needed to acknowledge that even though they had not been part of the Jewish nation, they too shared now in the promise of righteousness and justification first promised by God to Abraham and his offspring. Through faith in Christ.

Listen to Paul's words, which I believe support Paul's main theme throughout Romans.

Does this blessedness only apply for the circumcised or for the uncircumcised? Was it after (Abraham) was circumcised or before? It was not after but before! And he received the sign of circumcision, a seal of the righteousness that he had by faith while he was still uncircumcised. So then, he is the father of all who believe but have not been uncircumcised, in order that righteousness might be credited to them. And he is also the father of the circumcised who not only are circumcised but who also walked in the foot-steps of faith that our father Abraham had before he was circumcised. Therefore, the promise comes by faith, so that it may be by grace and may be guaranteed to all Abraham's offspring – not only to those who are of the law but also those who are of the faith of Abraham. He is the father of us all. (Rom. 4:9-12; 16).

Paul emphasized here that ultimate salvation comes from faith in Christ, not only by the works of the Old Testament Jewish law. His main point in Romans 4 is the exact opposite of what many use his words for - dividing Christian believers between an elect and a non-elect. Paul wrote to unite those who had always believed they were the elect (the Jews who were coming to Christ) and the newly elect (Gentiles who were coming to Christ) into one faith family. He tells the Gentiles they too have the same God of the Old Testament, and the same promise of righteousness from God, as the Jews enjoyed. He reassures the Gentiles that their ancestors, had they walked in whatever glimmer of faith in God they had, could have been considered by God to be part of the circumcised (the elect).

To the Jews, he reminded them clearly that the time for relying solely upon the Old Testament law (performing tasks) for salvation had ended, replaced in the fullness of time by faith in Jesus Christ, his Lord and our Lord.

Still, can we be certain Paul wrote in Romans 4 about Abraham's faith leading to his becoming the father of many nations (Jew and Gentile) instead of about Abraham's faith leading to his individual predestined salvation? Perhaps all we need to do is quote directly from Paul's words:

> Therefore, the promise comes by faith, so that it may be by grace and may be guaranteed to all Abraham's offspring—not only to those who are of the law but also to those who have the faith of Abraham. *He is the father of us all.* As it is written: "*I have made you a father of many nations.*" (Rom. 4:16-17)

5.2 Taking the Fifth

As we concluded the last section on Romans 4, I offered a lengthy passage to further support the claim that the Apostle's theme, including his discussion of Jacob and Esau in Romans 9, was to bring Jew and Gentile together in the new Christian Church. For today's Catholic, this means that any attempt by an Evangelical to separate us and our families off into the ranks of a predestined Reprobate is entirely untrue. Paul reminded his readers that God always had planned to offer the fellowship Abraham enjoyed with him to all peoples, now through Christ. This theme is displayed in a single verse which I left out of the section quoted above.

> Against all hope, Abraham in hope believed and so became the father of many nations. (Rom. 4:18)

This same theme is driven forward in Romans 5, despite the numerous Evangelical statements referencing that chapter as further support for the ideas we've defined in PIE. The first verse of the chapter is often used as a proof for the Reformation idea of 'Faith Alone' (sola fide),

> Therefore, since we have been justified through faith, we have peace with God through our Lord Jesus Christ, through whom we have gained access by faith into this grace in which we now stand. (Rom. 5:1-2)

Do these verses really mean we ONLY need faith? Paul refutes that assertion in the very next verse. He does not see eternal life in Christ coming only from a feeling that one possesses faith. He believed a Christ follower requires much more.

> Not only so, but we also glory in our suffer-
> ings, because we know that suffering produces per-
> severance; perseverance, character; and character,
> hope. And hope does not put us to shame, because
> God's love has been poured out into our hearts
> through the Holy Spirit, who has been given to us.
> (Rom. 5:3-5)

Paul did not see a momentary predestined regeneration as being enough for salvation. He understood that what believers do and experience, including suffering, builds within us those traits needed to remain a child of God. Not on our own, we notice, for God aides us by pouring his Spirit into our hearts. But neither by the Spirit working alone without us developing perseverance, character and hope.

Looking again at the flower defined by TULIP, Romans 5 is also used to support the idea of Total Depravity. The idea that we are all born by nature spiritually dead and only a God-driven, permanent regeneration of our Spirit can allow us to move in the slightest direction toward God. For we read Paul stating:

> You see, at just the right time, when we were still
> powerless, Christ died for the ungodly (Rom. 5:6)

"See?" we are asked. "Paul wrote that we are powerless.
What can that mean except that we are spiritually dead due to
our Total Depravity?"

And yet in the next verse Paul continued:

> You see, at just the right time, when we were still
> powerless, Christ died for the ungodly. Very rarely
> will anyone die for a **righteous** person, though for a
> good person someone might possibly dare to die.
> (Rom. 5:7)

"See?" we ask our Evangelical brother or sister in response, "Paul tells us right here that there are 'righteous'
people in the world. How can he do this if we are all born
Totally Depraved?"

In light of the entire context of Romans up to this point,
it seems more likely that Paul used the word 'powerless' here
to remind his Gentile readers that they, once cut off from the
Old Testament laws and promises, now had 'gained access'
(verse 1) to life with God through Christ.

Many Evangelicals have been taught what I call a 'sola'
mentality. In this, they believe there is only one meaning of
any specific word, verse or theme. So, when I above reminded
us that Paul stated there are righteous people, the immediate

response might be, "Are you saying that some people are born perfect (righteous)?"

The short answer is 'of course not.' Noticing that someone is living righteously does not imply they are perfect. But, for argument's sake, let's forget that Paul's comment about the existence of 'righteous' people seems to disprove the concept of Total Depravity. In the same verse, Paul also stated that there are sometimes 'good' people who recognize right from wrong and are willing to sacrifice themselves for those who are 'righteous.' Again, additionally strong proofs against the foundational doctrine underlying TULIP.

As we saw earlier, Evangelicals claim that Romans 3:11-12 proves that no one does good, not even one. But here, in Chapter 5, Paul says that people do sacrifice their lives for others. And Jesus told us that sacrificing oneself for another is the highest form of love. A love that, it would seem, casts fatal doubt upon Total Depravity.

In order to entirely 'beat this dead horse,' we then unearth another statement against the idea of Total Depravity in this chapter.

> But the gift is not like the trespass. For if the many died by the trespass of the one man, how much more did God's grace and the gift that came by the grace of the one man, Jesus Christ, overflow to the many!
>
> Consequently, just as one trespass resulted in condemnation for all people, so also one righteous

act resulted in justification and life for all people. (Rom. 5:15-18)

First, we notice the word 'many,' in verse 15, and not 'all.' 'All' could imply, as Evangelicals claim, that the nature of every single soul had been somehow changed. 'Many' could imply that those who choose to act like Adam acted, in pride and rebellion against God, will suffer the same fate.

In the second paragraph, Paul does use the word 'all.' Is this inconsistent with the previous verse? No, not if we understand, again, that Paul wrote to Jews and Gentiles. Here, he says not that Adam's sin universally condemned forever every individual human being, but that he brought condemnation to both groups of people Paul was writing to. This is shown again in the verses immediately preceding the two paragraphs shown above, when Paul confirms for his Gentile readers that their ancestors also suffered from the Fall even though they had no Old Testament Law to be judged against.

To be sure, sin was in the world before the law was given, but sin is not charged against anyone's account where there is no law. Nevertheless, death reigned from the time of Adam to the time of Moses, even over those who did not sin by breaking a command, as did Adam, who is a pattern of the one to come. (Rom. 5:13-14)

The final proof against the idea of Total Depravity in this section, however, comes from the work 'all' in verse 18. For if we interpret 'all' to mean all individuals, and that Adam's sin condemned 'all' to Total Depravity, then we also must interpret the remainder of the verse to mean that Jesus' work on the Cross has led to justification and life for 'all.' That every single human being born after Jesus has been born with souls that are now 'Totally Good.' And this, well, even those holding to the most ardently literal reading of scripture would reject such universalism.

5.3 Romans 6

I can with a clear conscience attend services on Sundays and listen to Evangelical Preaching during the week and meet with Evangelicals at ecumenical conferences simply because I believe Evangelicals are sincere Christ followers. In fact, my Catholic Church teaches explicitly that we consider all properly baptized Christians as being savable, though perhaps not benefiting from all that is offered by the faith left to us by Christ through his Apostles.

I initially dove into a review of the Book of Romans because I heard good-hearted Christian Pastors tell me and my children that we Catholics were unsaved (and worse). We were told we were not part of the elect of God. And we were told, mainly from the words written in Romans, that those who are part of God's elect have been predestined individually for salvation while all others have been chosen to suffer in hell – each without regard to anything they did or said or thought.

As I moved through chapter 5 and 6 of his letter to Rome, I noticed that Paul pointed out to his readers the great benefits God provides us through Christ. He argued that God had a plan to counteract the sin of Adam, to turn our condemnation into righteousness through Jesus. I see this to mean that God created us with human-will, even knowing that due to this human-will, we would certainly fall into sin. Knowing this, he (Father, Son, and Holy Spirit) planned to heal our sins and provide the opportunity for salvation through Christ in the fullness of time. Those who sought, accepted, and nurtured their faith would benefit from this predetermined plan. The individual who joined this community of Christ-followers would share in the predestined path for salvation.

Those who entered this community of believers Paul wrote to became part of this new elect. But the election was not individually predetermined but granted to the Christian family as a whole. Individually, based upon our choices and faith, we could either enter or leave this family. God's mercy, justice and loving nature would be maintained, as would his Sovereign Will and all-powerful nature. Call this reality, perhaps, the *communal* predestined election of Christians.

The differences between this Communal Predestined Election (CPE) of the Christian faithful versus Predestined Individual Election are significant in practice. CPE supports the idea that God calls and welcomes all people to this community. Jesus suffered, died and rose again to enable all people to join his family, both here and in the next life. We can reach out and love all people, for we know that each of us is equally responsible and capable of making the right choices to come best we can to God as Lord and Savior. In contrast, individual predestination tends to completely divide people between those who have had no choice but to be saved from those who have had no choice but to remain outside God's love.

That said, we are getting closer to the key chapter of Romans 9. Will we now begin to find any direct support for the exclusive interpretation leading to Predestined Individual Election?

Paul knew that some within the Christian community, when reading his letter emphasizing the grace now being offered to Jew and Gentile alike to supersede the Old Testament law, might interpret his words as giving license to sin. That a mistaken reading of his words to mean 'faith alone' would convince some that their sins no longer mattered. Paul spent much of Romans 6 stating over and over that nothing was further from his purpose. Sin, he says, still matters very much in our lives with God.

What shall we say, then? Shall we go on sinning so that grace may increase? By no means! We are those who have died to sin; how can we live in it any longer? (Rom. 6:1-2)

As we saw in Romans 5 when Paul compared Adam's impact on the human race with the impact of our Lord Jesus, we find in Romans 6 a discussion concerning the impact of sin against the righteousness. Evangelicals sometimes focus on the verse where we read, "When you were slaves to sin, you were free from the control of righteousness" (Rom. 6:20) to again promote the idea of Total Depravity. But they ignore Paul's words two verses later, "But now that you have been set free from sin and have become slaves of God, the benefit you reap leads to holiness, and the result is eternal life" (Rom. 6:22).

We cannot say that we are 'slaves' to sin, in other words powerless against it, when Paul then tells us we are now 'slaves' to God. Not when our slavery to God still includes our tendency to sin. Our free human-will choice to sin.

So, are we still, as believers in Christ (and therefore Regenerate according to Calvinist thought), free and driven to sin? Paul tells us exactly this in Romans 7.

5.4 Romans 7

Paul begins Romans 7 writing again to his Jewish brethren about the burdens they used to carry while under the Old Testament Law. He uses the analogy of a spouse being freed from of their spousal commitments after the death of their loved one. Similarly, he then writes that they, the Jewish Christians, have 'died to the Law through the body of Christ' (Rom. 7:4). Having died with Christ, they are no longer under the Law but are instead free to serve God directly through Christ and the Holy Spirit.

He goes into great length to demonstrate to his fellow Jews that while the Old Testament law was valuable and necessary, it did not keep him or anyone else from sinning. In fact, he says, the law made him sin and covet all the more, stressing to anyone still looking for salvation through that old path that it is a useless endeavor, and redemption can only come through Christ.

Indeed, I would not have known what sin was except through the law. For I would not have known what coveting really was if the law had not said, "Do not covet." But sin, seizing the opportunity afforded by the commandment, produced in me every kind of covetous desire. (Rom. 7:8)

Paul adds to that, "When I want to do good, evil is right there with me. For in my inner being I delight in God's law, but I see another law at work in the members of my body." (Rom. 7:21-23)

I've heard many Evangelical Preachers say – "See? Paul says here that he wants to do good but even he cannot. He knew we are all dead in our sins. He is confirming that we are Totally Depraved."

In fact, for Paul to say this puts us at odds more with Irresistible Grace and the Perseverance of the Saints that it places us under the heal of Total Depravity.

But I believe there is a much more obvious and simple explanation for Paul's words. He continues by writing what I can summarize as, "I know firsthand that through our own efforts, even following the Law to the highest degree, we cannot succeed. We all need Christ."

What about this idea that the Law is making him sin? Perhaps we can imagine a midnight buffet on a cruise ship. A pile of every dessert ever made sits before us. We see that table of sweets and perhaps we feel a deep rumble in our bellies. But then…well, then we read the sign at the beginning of the line for that spread. Emblazoned on the placard before the most mouthwatering photo of a chocolate cake ever snapped, we read, 'Please do not overindulge on our moist and delicious desserts. They are fattening and can lead to heart disease.'

Tell me, will any one of us resist the temptation of that gooey chocolate cake? The sign was correct and valuable and meant to help us, as did God's Old Testament commands and restrictions. But reminded by the sign of the available temptation, we in our weakness will give in and eat the cake. Perhaps this is the warning Paul gave his contemporaries – 'I studied the restrictions of the Law and found myself ever more tempted and covetous.'

But if we look at that chocolate cake and think about Jesus, and how he wants us to enjoy our lives in good health and that he sacrificed so much for us, might we then be more able to resist? Might we be free of this temptation? Might we, even if we do give in, benefit from his forgiveness for our gluttonous ways?

Paul says as much, "Who will rescue me from this body of death? Thanks be to God – through Jesus Christ our Lord" (Rom. 7:24-25). This is not a prayer for escape from the body but a victory over it.

As we mentioned above, another item that must be addressed before moving from these verses is this: TULIP teaches that the elect receive irresistible grace and a regenerate soul. If true, then how – among all of humanity – can the Apostle Paul maintain that he still has evil within him? And not only that he continues to bear evil within him, but that he succumbs to it and sin. And, that these sins still matter with regard to his eternal life?

> What a wretched man I am! Who will rescue me
> from this body that is subject to death? Thanks be to
> God, who delivers me through Jesus Christ our Lord!
> (Rom. 7:24-25)

5.5 Luther's Moment

We began our look at Romans by studying several key verses in Romans 9 that have used to surmise that every human being is born with a nature set entirely against our creator. The idea that Paul used the characters of Jacob and Esau to defend the idea that one was loved through a predestined plan, while the other was hated, has been exposed as an error. Instead, these well-known Old Testament characters coincided with Paul's comparison of the Jewish and Gentile nations before Christ.

We then came to understand that Paul's references to the Prophet Malachi and the Book of Psalms earlier in Romans cannot be read in a vacuum if we hope to determine the proper interpretation of his words. Taking, for example, a single verse which claims no one does good cannot prove Total Depravity if the very next Psalm states that there are those who can and do live righteously.

When the first Reformers, beginning with Martin Luther, sought to break away from the Church, they had to develop the idea that the Church's teaching, practices, activities, and sacraments were useless, at best, and soul-destroying at worst. Luther and the others found in Total Depravity the perfect doctrine to convince potential converts that no one could ever follow any set of requirements set down by the Church, and therefore those requirements could not represent the proper pathway to Christ.

Once the Reformers defined this new understanding concerning our core natures (as we read in Luther's major work, The Bondage of the Will (1525)), then the only hope for the Christian is to move away from any practices of the Church and toward *sola fide* – faith alone. But not a faith which we develop through study and discipline (which would again point back to the community of the Church and individual choice), but through God's intervention alone into some of our individual souls.

Luther needed to convince himself, and potential followers, that the only thing which did matter, the one thing that could still save when the framework of the Church was gone, was faith. Faith alone.

Luther found support for his new idea from his reading of Romans. During what has become known as his 'Tower Experience,' Luther read this in Romans 1:

> For in the gospel the righteousness of God is revealed—a righteousness that is by faith from first to last, just as it is written: "The righteous will live by faith." (Rom. 1:17)

Some maintain that this was the moment for Luther, and not his posting of the 95 Theses, that was the practical start of the Reformation. Luther himself wrote about this moment,

> 'The just person lives by faith.' (Rom 1:17) All at once I felt that I had been born again and entered into paradise itself through open gates.[5]

Those who believe in the doctrines we defined as PIE maintain from this statement, 'The righteous will live by faith', that there are a chosen few individuals who will 'live' spiritually while all others remain spiritually 'dead' – and this 'life' is established only upon faith. The dead who God regenerates to life will live by their new faith and receive the eternal blessings of the righteous.

However, there is one more obvious and consistent interpretation of this verse as well. Let's read it again.

"The righteous will live by faith."

In other words, there are those considered righteous (remember, Paul stated that in Romans 5, as we reviewed above), and these righteous people live in a certain way. They live their lives through faith - faith in God, in his commandments, and who God really is. If Jesus is the Lord creator of the universe, then he is truly our God and must be obeyed. If Christ is Savior of mankind, then he must also be trusted for forgiveness should we humbly repent in light of Jesus' atoning sacrifice. This is how the 'righteous live by faith.' We live our lives guided by what we believe.

Once again, we need only look at the Old Testament verse Paul quoted from.

> See, the enemy is puffed up; his desires are not upright—but the righteous person will live by his faithfulness. (Hab. 2:4)

Notice the slightly different word here, 'Faithfulness'? Faithfulness is not only a state of mind, or a belief, or a feeling. Faithfulness is faith in action, a way of living and acting. Paul is not saying in verse seventeen that those who one day wake up and find themselves believing are then saves solely by that faith. The Apostle is repeating the theme of Habakkuk, that we LIVE (think, do and act), BY (guided by) FAITH. We live faithfully.

We know this interpretation is true because in the very next verse Paul contrasts this 'life guided by faith' with those who have rejected God and continue to live immorally.

> The wrath of God is being revealed from heaven against all the godlessness and wickedness of people, who suppress the truth by their wickedness, since what may be known about God is plain to them, because God has made it plain to them. For since the creation of the world God's invisible qualities—his eternal power and divine nature—have been clearly seen, being understood from what has been made, so that people are without excuse.
>
> For although they knew God, they neither glorified him as God nor gave thanks to him, but their thinking became futile and their foolish hearts were darkened. Although they claimed to be wise, they became fools. (Rom 1: 18-22)

As a final note, let us notice that while Paul here speaks about the 'godlessness and wickedness' of the people, this is not defending the idea of Total Depravity, but describes their non-faith-guided lives. This is clearly shown when Paul wrote, 'since what may be known about God is plain to them, because God has made it plain to them.' And, 'that people are without excuse.'

Nothing would be a better excuse for the sinful than to have been burdened with irresistible depravity from birth due simply with how their creator created them. Being 'without excuse' only makes sense if people can recognize and follow the ways of God, which he has made plain to all.

5.6 The 8-Ball

Many of us as children played with a sphere painted like a billiard's 8-ball. You would ask a question, perhaps, 'Was I chosen at the beginning of time by God to be elect,' and then flip the ball over to see your arbitrary answer floating before your eyes.

The concepts of Unconditional Election found in TULIP, when explained through Predestined Individual Election, demand that the answer to our salvation, or damnation, is simply the result of God's cosmic coin-flip. Some Catholics and Protestants have reconciled the seeming unfairness with our view of God's love, mercy, and righteousness. They say that God 'predestined' only in terms of being outside time itself and therefore witnessing our future decisions, actions and faith in his eternal 'now.' What may be seen from our end as an arbitrary fate that we cannot avoid is provided for us based upon what God knows we will do (and to him 'have done') in our lives.

This, however, is unacceptable to Evangelicals, who see in this middle ground a denial of God's sovereign will expressed in his choices to save or damn us on an individual level regardless of what we might do. Instead, Reformed theologians go to Romans 8 to propose God's step-by-step, irresistible plan for each elect individual. They point to what is commonly referred to as the 'Golden Chain.'

> And we know that in all things God works for the good of those who love him, who have been called according to his purpose. For those God foreknew he also predestined to be conformed to the image of his Son, that he might be the first-born among many brothers and sisters. And those he predestined, he also called; those he called, he also justified; those he justified, he also glorified. (Rom 8:28-30)

In these verses, we see Paul use the words 'foreknew' and 'predestined.' Two of the three words in PIE.

Have we perhaps missed something?

No.

Entering Chapter 8, Paul continued the theme we reviewed in Romans 1:17, that we Christ-followers are to live our lives as guided by the Holy Spirit.

Those who live according to the flesh have their minds set on what the flesh desires; but those who live in accordance with the Spirit have their minds set on what the Spirit desires. (Rom. 8:5)

Paul makes the point here that all believers are capable, and obligated, of living (guided by the Holy Spirit) a righteous life that they were unable to live without Christ.

Therefore, brothers and sisters, we have an *obligation* – but it is not to the sinful nature, to live according to it. (Rom. 8:12)

Paul wrote that we have an *obligation* to make the correct 'if' choices throughout our lives, and from that obedience will come the '*then*' - God's promise of salvation.

5.7 Breaking the Chain

But let us not bypass the Golden Chain so quickly. Let us read again what I have read and heard in hundreds of sermons and talks.

For those God foreknew he also predestined to be conformed to the image of his Son, that he might be the firstborn among many brothers and sisters. And those he predestined, he also called; those he called,

he also justified; those he justified, he also glorified.
(Rom. 8:29-30)

Do not these verses show that God foreknew which individuals he would predestine for his call, and from his call those individuals who would receive justification, and from their justification the individuals who will enjoy ultimate glory?

One can certainly decipher some of the doctrines of TULIP by reading these verses alone. But that is the problem. These verses, like all verses in the Bible, do not sit alone. They need to be read in context.

In this case, Romans 8:29-30 can only be properly understood in light of the preceding verse.

And we know that in all things God works for the good of *those who love* him. (Rom 8:28).

It is not a set of predetermined individual souls who receive the blessed fate defined by the Golden Chain. Those who are glorified are those who 'love' God. But who 'loves' God?

Jesus told us himself:

If you love me, *keep my commands.* (Jn. 14:15)
All well and good, as a possible alternative interpretation.

But which view of Romans 8:28-30 is correct? Can we not claim that 'those who love him' are only those who were once Totally Depraved and now find themselves regenerate?

The short answer is – not if we look at the context of Romans 8 or our real-world experiences.

If Paul here writes only of a group of individuals who are now regenerated and capable of only loving God through obedience, then there would be no need for warnings or encouragement. According to TULIP, these individuals now possess souls turned irresistibly toward God, and God will preserve them within their heaven-bound fates until the end, no matter what. But, instead, Paul wrote:

> Therefore, brothers and sisters, we have an obligation—but it is not to the flesh, to live according to it. For if you live according to the flesh, you will die; but if by the Spirit you put to death the misdeeds of the body, you will live. (Rom. 8:12-13)

Paul writes to those he considers 'brothers and sisters' and tells them that they still have an 'if/then' scenario before them. If they – believers in Christ – choose to 'live according to the flesh,' they will die. But, if they choose to proceed guided by the Spirit, they will live. The entry point (loving God) that defines the Golden Chain is not a reflection of a permanent state an individual finds themselves in, but motivation for each person to strive for continual obedience and love, leading to justification and eventually to glory in heaven.

Chapter 6

Young Catholic Eyes

When I attended church-school as a third and fourth grader, we received pocket-sized bibles. I remember how incredibly thin the paper was. How shiny. And how tiny the words. None of us at that age read them.

While a fourth grader in public school, I was also given a small booklet by one of my classmates. It contained page after page of black and white cartoons. These drawings, however, were not like the Saturday morning cartoons we watched, they were instead deadly serious. They showed snippets of the eternal future of a man, and the story struck home for me because this character was supposed to be a fellow Catholic. And he was clearly, desperately lost – eventually shown burning in hell.

I felt uneasy when I read the pamphlet and looked at the torment on the face of this man who was trying to live a good life and do everything he thought he needed to do to make it to heaven. When he died, the man's eyes were then dark hallows in a skeleton-like face, cowering before the brilliance of God set upon his throne. The man's left arm was raised, black and white tatters of his shirtsleeve hanging down before his face, receiving no respite from the vengeance of the Lord.

I didn't then understand as much of the symbolism as I do now, but I remember every picture had dark, angry, and billowing clouds or even tongues of fire surrounding the man. God sat opposing him in flowing robes, his face a simple clear oval because, as I later discovered, the Evangelical artist who drew the cartoon did not want to create an 'idol' by providing any detail to God's face.

I whispered many discussions in the back of our classroom with my friend. He probably didn't know much more about what the booklet preached than I; he was simply doing what his parents or Pastor commanded. He was, of course, just 'loving' his fellow human being and gave me this comic book so I would understand the truth about my 'evil' Pope who led me and my family toward predestined, individual damnation because we, of course, were Catholics who supposedly didn't believe in Christ as our savior.

It was just after this time, as I entered fifth grade, that I was assigned a new church-school teacher. I don't remember her name, but she was one of the nuns at the church, an older lady who did a very good job teaching us unruly and pre-hormonal brats. The church-school class was held each Wednesday afternoon, and sometimes I did not have a ride, but I would still walk the two miles or so from our house to the church to attend.

At some point, I must have won some sort of class contest

because the nun dug into her clearly empty pockets and presented me with my first real Bible. It had a blue cover and a large title, 'The Way.' Inside the Bible, there were many photos of teenagers, which I found fascinating as a child. Next to the photos were notes that said things like, "When you feel confused," "when you are sad," and so forth. Next to each note were three or four references to Bible verses that discussed those specific issues.

Perhaps most importantly, my new Bible included a simple recommendation – read one chapter per day, and three on Sundays. I don't recall for sure if the editors proposed where to start, but my mind's eye remembers a reading plan which started with Mark, then Acts, Galatians, Genesis and then Exodus.

And so, I and my fifth-grade brain set off with the task of reading one chapter per day no matter what. I continued this practice almost every day without fail until I went off to college. I wonder sometimes if the boy who gave me those highly damning cartoon books in fourth grade ever spent as much time within the Holy Scriptures as I, a young Catholic, did.

But read and read I did, occasionally wading through the 'boring' parts like the Old Testament lists of rituals and rulers and tribes and genealogies. I was of course *doing*, in the words of today's Evangelical, a 'work' and, yes, I did begin to feel somewhat disconcerted (sinful?) on those few days I failed to keep up with my reading. Perhaps, since it was the 'work' of reading and studying scripture, my Evangelical friends will make an exception. Perhaps this work is not actually a work, and maybe we should all feel like we are doing something wrong if we don't read God's word each day – whether we call it a work or not? For this work kept me, at least, growing in faith. Just like my daily prayers. Just like my weekend Mass.

6.1 Galatians

When I made it into middle school, which we called 'junior high' in upstate New York, I reread (though it seemed like my first reading due to the impact it made upon me) the book of Galatians. Up to that point, I spent most of my time reading either the Gospels or the more well-known Old Testament books like Exodus. Perhaps the books of theology written by Paul were simply too deep for me at an earlier age.

The stories of Jesus, however, absolutely fascinated me, and while we were never taught to memorize chapter and verse, I found myself being changed from the inside out due to my daily interface with Christ. For a long season, I took the words of Jesus literally and with great hope when he said we would be given anything we asked for in faith. I prayed during school pretty much between every class for a certain young lady to ask me out (because as I lacked the nerve to ask her).

It sounds very silly now to engage the Lord's direct help in such puppy love, but the habit of this constant prayer became one of the greatest blessings of my life. I'm reminded of *It's a Wonderful Life*, when George Bailey looks to heaven in absolute distress while at the bar, saying, "I'm not a praying man but…'. He was a wonderful character, a loving and caring soul. But such a desperate, lonely waste of so many years. A good man lacking prayer, lacking in communication with his Lord.

My first foray beyond the New Testament Gospels was within the Book of Acts. I love history and found this retelling of the growth of the early church invigorating, although I remember being disappointed in how abruptly the Book of Acts ended. What came next, I wondered? Beyond the Apostles – us, I suppose – and all of our stories.

I dipped my toes into the waters of the Apostle Paul and did find him addressing 'us,' in terms of dealing with the real-life issues facing the early Christian church. Unfortunately, when first reading his self-defense in Second Corinthians, 10:23, I stumbled across, "Are they servants of Christ? I know I sound like a madman, but I have served him far more! I have worked harder, been put in prison more often, been whipped times without number, and faced death again and again."

My young mind missed the Apostle's sarcasm and found Paul to be off-putting and somewhat egotistical. When I finally understood the background of his words in that section, I realized how important it is to not lead someone blindly into the scriptures. Instead, we should make every effort to provide the new Bible reader the proper context and a plan. Not a list of cherry-picked verses cobbled together to prove a desired theology, but a plan, for example, to begin with one of the Gospels (of course, for the entire goal is to learn about Christ), then selected Old Testament readings that teach us about God and his plan for salvation, then perhaps Acts to demonstrate how the early church dealt with the most amazing fact in human history – the Resurrection of Christ.

Eventually, I overcame my negativity against Paul (since we Catholics read from his writings during many, if not most, Sunday Masses), and read his words to the Galatians. Suddenly, I felt as if my eyes were totally opened to a more personal relationship with Jesus. I don't know exactly what I read. I don't know which part of that book stood out for me. But it energized my faith life for a long period of time. It gave me a deeper Catholic faith as Paul's words also brought alive my experience within the Church and the Mass.

Later in life, then, it came as something of a slap in the face to hear so many references from my Evangelical preacher friends to the book of Galatians for support of their ideas concerning Predestined Individual Election. They applied Paul's words to these early Christ-followers to claim one group of Christians belong to an elect group, and all the rest do not.

So, as I spent time with my children in our Evangelical setting, reopened my Bible to Galatians, and kept in mind what I had now read and reread in Romans, and tried to discern what Paul wrote in this shorter letter, and if his words really supported the Calvinistic reading of Paul's letter to Rome.

Paul did not *need* to have the same theme in each of his books beyond, of course, the saving power of Christ and the importance of the Gospel. But it would be fascinating if in the same book Evangelicals find similarities with Romans, I also could find similarities supporting what I had concluded was Paul's true theme in his letter to Rome. If the Apostle's main thrust for Rome was answering questions being raised about the relationship between the Jews and Gentiles within the new Christian Church, maybe he expressed similar thoughts to the church in Galatia.

A particularly clear tie to Romans is found in Galatians 4. Paul again uses Old Testament characters as his example, just as he had used Jacob and Esau in the book of Romans to represent the Jewish and Gentile peoples before Christ. My ears perked up when I discovered a similar discussion in Galatians concerning the Old Testament characters Hagar and Sarah, the mothers of two of Abraham's children.

Paul once again addresses his Jewish readers who still clung to their customs and laws which previously identified their community as the chosen elect.

Tell me, you who want to be under the law, are you not aware of what the law says? For it is written that Abraham had two sons....(one) born in the ordinary way, but his son by the free women was born as the result of a promise. (Gal. 4:21)

Paul not only develops his theme with the example of two women, Sarah and Hagar, just as in Romans he used Jacob and Esau, but in the very next verses, he clarifies that "These things may be taken *figuratively*, for these women *represent two covenants.*" (Gal. 4:24)

If St. Paul is addressing the topic of unifying Jew and Gentile within the new Christian church in Galatia, and he tells us explicitly that he used two Old Testament characters to represent those ancient groups, would it not make sense that he also used the Old Testament characters in Romans 9 not as individuals but as figuratively representing two covenants?

If Paul referenced Jacob and Esau as representatives of the Jewish and Gentile nations, then his assertion that God chose one to love meant not that he loved and predestined Jacob as an individual for salvation but that he loved and predestined the group the man represented, the Old Testament Jews. This elect group's relationship with God was being transferred to the new Christian church, offering salvation through Christ.

In the second half of the verse mentioned above, he continued;

...for the women represent two covenants. One covenant is from Mount Sinai and bears children who are to be slaves: This is Hagar. Now Hagar stands for Mount Sanai in Arabia and corresponds to the present city of Jerusalem, because she is in slavery with her children. But the Jerusalem that is above and is free, and she, Sarah, is our mother. (Gal. 4:24-26)

Paul explicitly tells his Jewish readers in Galatia – who would be familiar with the Old Testament account in Genesis, that Hagar (who they would have thought represented the Gentiles) represented those contemporary Jews still 'enslaved' to the present city of Jerusalem with its Old Testament laws and rituals. In contrast, Sarah and now represented the new elect, those who have entered the Jerusalem that is above and free. They – whether previously Jew of Gentile – who now follow Christ.

So in Christ Jesus you are all children of God through faith, for all of you who were baptized into Christ have clothed yourselves with Christ. There is neither Jew nor Gentile. (Gal. 3:26-28)

Paul stressed that Christians, through the freedom gained by Christ, are saved through faith, and are represented by Sarah, while those who were still Jewish and trying to follow the Old Testament laws to gain righteousness are represented by the example of Hagar.

This, of course, supports the idea that Paul is using the same figurative, and 'communal,' sense while writing

Romans, and there used the Old Testament heroes of Jacob and Esau as fill-ins for each group. God has, it would seem, created a plan for all, Gentile or Jew, who choose to follow the path into the community of the elect, the new Christian Church.

Just a few sentences later in Galatians, Paul repeats the use of familiar Old Testament characters, writing to Jewish and Gentile Christian readers alike:

> Now you brothers, *like Isaac,* are children of promise. (Gal. 4:28)

Here it is! Exactly what Paul wrote to the Romans. That salvation transcends Jacob (the Jews) or Esau (the Gentiles) to their father in the faith, Isaac.

> Nor because they are his descendants are they all Abraham's children. On the contrary, "It is through Isaac that your offspring will be reckoned." (Rom. 9:7)

Paul wrote his letter to Rome, and in that massive capital city of the Empire, the new Christian church contained a blend of Jew and Gentile. He used Jacob and Esau to represent both Jewish and Gentile nations, demonstrating to both groups that God had been fair to each and called them equally to salvation through Jesus. Paul wanted them to move beyond their Jewish or Gentile identities and become one family in Christ.

In Galatia, the major issue was that new Christians with Gentile backgrounds were being challenged by Jews who forced upon them the rules of the Old Testament. To address and fix this error, Paul again uses the well-known stories of the Old Testament for his proofs, reminding his Jewish readers that the new elect – Christians – did not need to follow the Laws of the old elect. To do so, he went back in redemptive history beyond the Jew (Jacob) and Gentile (Esau) to identify common ground, and common spiritual descent, from their father, Isaac.

The Old Testament Law was most readily associated with the act of circumcision. Clearly, the Gentile Christians were being pressured by the Jewish Christians to become physically circumcised in adherence with their traditional practices. Paul addressed this issue directly, "If you let yourselves be circumcised Christ will be of no value to you at all." (Gal. 5:2)

Paul had gone to great lengths to bring Gentiles to Christ in Galatia and elsewhere. He worked hard explaining to former Jews the salvation due to faith in Christ, freeing them from the ceremonial precepts of the Old Testament. Now, he learned that some were being pulled away from the faith by those still trying to enforce the Old Testament. The tasks assigned by the Old Testament, while important to maintain the Jewish faith through the centuries preceding Christ, did not have the power to save by themselves. Paul reminds his readers of this: "The only thing that counts is faith expressing itself *through love*" (Gal. 5:6).

But, again, let's not confuse the idea of Old Testament 'tasks' and Christian 'works' of love. The idea of faith '*expressing itself through love*' here does not refer to a simple *feeling* of love toward one another, but (as we will later read in the words of James as well) the expression of love through kind and charitable works.

Paul even shares with his readers the time he had to confront Peter, and he writes to the Galatians that, "I said to Peter in front of them all, 'You are a Jew, yet you live like a Gentile and not like a Jew. How is it then that you force Gentiles to follow Jewish customs?'" (Gal. 2:14)

Peter had led the Christian leadership in Acts 15 to determine the Old Testament Jewish laws were no longer required. Under the pressure of others coming from Jerusalem, however, he acquiesced to these 'Judaizers' who insisted God still demanded that the old ways needed to be followed. Paul, desperate to bring Jews and Gentiles together equally, reminded Peter of this, a theme he carries through all of Galatians.

6.2 Ephesians

Paul also wrote to the infant church in Ephesus, and in the second chapter we're presented another of the supposed proof points of Predestined Individual Election. In Ephesians

2:8-9, Paul states, 'For it is by grace you have been saved, through faith – and this is not from yourselves, it is a gift from God – not by works, so that no one can boast."

This verse is interpreted by Evangelicals to mean we do nothing to help nor hinder our salvation, but God alone (as a 'gift' provided to some) has already decided to whom to provide salvation through grace. His sovereignty is defended by Paul who states here that since we can do nothing ('works' from ourselves), we cannot boast. As we discussed earlier, the words in these two verses, carved out by themselves, can logically be used to support the Reformed case.

However, coming now from a growing sense built upon Romans and Galatians that there was a different theme running through Paul's mind. Let's continue within Ephesians to see if the other themes proposed in this book revealed themselves here as well.

Following Eph. 2:8-9, Paul goes immediately back to the recurring theme we've sensed in his other writings; 'this mystery is that through the Gospel, the Gentiles are heirs together with Israel, members together of one body, and sharers together in the promise of Christ Jesus' (Eph. 3:6).

Note that he did *not* say, 'individual Gentiles and Jews chosen from all eternity past,' but instead the implication is that there are some from both of these Old Testament groups who are now in the new community of Christians, sharing in the promise of Jesus. He could not have meant, as can be literally read, that ALL Gentiles are heirs with ALL Jews

either, so we must assume Paul meant only that the opportunity now exists for the faithful and obedient from both
groups to be saved. Those from either group had once sinned
equally, and not they were equally called to faithfulness
through Jesus.

He continues the idea of the equality of Jew and Gentile
in the very next section:

> Therefore, remember that formerly you who are
> Gentiles by birth and called 'uncircumcised' by those
> who call themselves 'the circumcision', remember
> that at that time you were separate from Christ...but
> now in Christ Jesus, you who were once far away
> have been brought near by the blood of Christ. (Eph.
> 2:11-13)

We are then brought fully back to the theme we found in
Romans, as Paul treats again the most pressing issue of his
time,

> ...for he himself is our peace, who has *made the two
> groups one and destroyed the barrier*, the dividing
> wall of hostility by setting aside in his flesh the law
> with its commands and regulations. He came and
> preached peace to you who were far away (Gentiles)
> and peace to those who were near (Jews). For
> through him we both have access to the Father by one

Spirit. (Eph. 2:14, 17, words in paratheses added)

Paul did not include in his 'not by works,' the works of the moral law, however. In chapters four and five, the Apostle gave detailed instructions for how members within the Body of Christ should live. He also confirmed that our ongoing sins against the moral law (verses the Jewish ceremonial laws) matter with regards to our eternal communion with God:

> No immoral, impure or greedy person—such a person is an idolater—has any inheritance in the kingdom of Christ and of God. Let no one deceive you with empty words, for because of such things God's wrath comes on those who are disobedient. (Eph 5:5-6)

Could Paul, when he wrote, 'and this is not from yourselves, it is a gift from God – not by works, so that no one can boast' (Eph. 2:9) simply be telling his Jewish-Christian readers that their boasting of obedience to the Old Testament ceremonial laws meant nothing compared to the Father's gift of Christ? Is he, here again, reflecting upon the idea that it is this new *community* of believers which is predestined - through a sovereign plan created by the Father since before time – to be brought to salvation through Christ *if* they (regardless of religious background) – *choose* to enter this new family and follow the Lord?

Chapter 7

Taking a Breath

A thought occurred to me –

The death of Jesus is all that was needed for our justification, but the crucifixion and resurrection were required for our sanctification.

There are many theories concerning how the sacrifice of our Lord cures us of the penalty for our sins. Does the Cross remove our sins? Does it hide them? Does God simply choose to ignore our failings, or are we completely healed from our sinful nature and prevented from becoming spiritually sick again? Did Jesus die on Calvary in humble obedience to counter the pride of Adam in his sin? Was Jesus publicly crucified to provide a model of divine forgiveness?

The debate continues.

7.1 The difficulty with PIE

One idea seems to be generally accepted, however, is that we are all less than holy and deserve punishment for our sins. God came among us as a man, and he sacrificed his own life so we can be healed from our spiritual death. Jesus told us himself that such a sacrifice (one's life for the life of others) is the height and depth of love. Paul compared Jesus' humility on the Cross as a direct opposite of Adam's choice to disobey God in the garden.

But why, I have often wondered, did Jesus need to die as he did, hanging and tortured upon the Cross? If Predestined Individual Election (PIE) is true, then God planned to provide a certain group of individuals forgiveness of their sins by granting them the unconditional and irresistible grace needed to overcome their inherent Total Depravity and *desire* fellowship again with God. To facilitate this desire, it is easy to see that Christ would be part of the plan, coming to earth as a man to provide a critical link for us to the Father. Faith in Christ would essentially be faith in the Father, only easier for us material human beings to understand.

That explains the Incarnation, perhaps, but again, why the Cross?

We can claim, of course, that there are two steps necessary for salvation. First, we humans had to establish a relationship with God which was made possible through a fellow 'man.' Second, since God is a just God, he could not simply ignore our sins. The guilt had to be paid for. Justice had to be served. Perhaps we can make the case that God could have chosen anything as propitiation (payment) for the sins of the elect, but he in his sovereign will chose the death penalty, the washing of our sins in the blood of his Son.

But, all this required was Jesus' death. A private beheading, like that of John, would have sufficed. So, again, why the Cross?

The Cross is a reminder, a motivation, an example of one who had all the power of God still humbling himself before the Father. Christ's entire life, in fact, was not just to show us his God-ness, but it was also to show us how to live in proper humility as a human being. Once we are justified (forgiven) of our sins through baptism and enter a state of saving grace, we are all called to continue our walk with Christ and grow in goodness and faith (sanctification). For now, let us ignore any debate over whether we could ever turn our back on God (or is his grace 'irresistible')? Let us even ignore the consequences of failing in our walk of faith (i.e., do we lose our state of salvation, or are we 'once saved, always saved'?), the bottom line is we all understand the faithful should act in ways pleasing our Father.

The process of our sanctification is what the very public, very painful, and very humiliating crucifixion was really for. Christ died as he did to enable us to truly believe in his love. He could have died poisoned in his sleep. He could have died on one of his prayerful night walks. He only needed to die for us to benefit from a path toward justification. Although the Father didn't need the torture or the blood of his Son, *we did,* for it was through that suffering that we realize the true depth of Christ's love.

Upon the Cross, that shameful humiliating cross, Jesus demonstrated for us the proper position of humility, trust, and reliance upon the Father. Upon the Cross, in his moment of agony, he also modeled for us a level of forgiveness that we could not have understood through a thousand parables. Upon the Cross, he showed us that we all need to repent for the very sins that caused him to be raised upon that tree in the first place.

The problem with Predestined Individual Election is that the doctrine maintains, no matter what, that God chose to save only those few he will save, and no others. If so, then it can certainly be argued Jesus' death was not necessary, for the Father could have made any random state of our existence the determining factor in our salvation.

To my Catholic ears, hearing that the elect had been determined to be so since all eternity-past, regardless of their choices or actions or attempts to grow in sanctification, seemed to remove the very purpose of the Cross itself. If God chose to save the elect through some state they find themselves in, that state could just as easily have been the possession of red hair or a pleasing singing voice.

The basic, and somewhat troubling question is – if not one person who was chosen to be elect then lost their faith because of the Cross and resurrection, and not one person who was denied the saving grace of election came to Christ and benefited in any way from the Cross then...you got it, why the Cross at all?

Just as troubling for me as I delved deeper into Calvinist thought, while I see how some can conclude only a belief in Predestined Individual Election protects our view of God's omnipotence, the doctrine causes overwhelming damage to our concept of his love, his fairness, and his mercy. As a father, I cannot grasp a theology that demands that our loving Father could ever decide, no matter what I or my children believe or say or do, that one or more of us are already damned to the torments of hell from the very beginning of time.

7.2 The Effect on Evangelization

When I was solely living a Catholic life, I didn't think much about evangelization. I often hear people quote St. Francis that we are always to preach the Gospel to those around us, and sometimes even use our words. That statement is quite profound and allows us to focus on the idea that our life in Christ should be visible through our actions as much as through our words.

However, I also now realize that the attitude we may develop by taking this approach is lazy. We decide not to use our words, not to reach out, not to do the hard and sometimes scary work of sharing God with others. In the Christian society we now live in, our culture expects people to behave a certain way, so our actions alone are no longer enough to make someone realize what God has done in our lives.

I once travelled to Singapore for business. Our local Singaporean manager met me at the hotel restaurant for breakfast. It was served buffet style, and I filled my plate first and sat down. I waited, patiently, as a plate of bacon beaconed me from below. My host returned to the table maybe five minutes later. He looked at my untouched plate for a moment and then put his napkin upon his lap. He looked at me and asked, "Are you a Christian?"

I wonder if anyone in America would take notice of such simple actions on my part as waiting for him to arrive at the table before eating. Would anyone in our society assume my actions were due to my Christian faith?

More importantly, though, the essential teachings of Christianity are not only a set of actions. We do not simply want others to mimic our activities, although if we are true to our faith our own Christian works will improve over time. No, our faith is primarily one of belief, of humbly repenting of our sins and following the Lord. These things cannot be properly understood by non-believers simply by looking at our outward actions.

Actions matter. Words matter even more. Explanations of our words, explaining our faith and life in Jesus Christ, matter the most.

What is the Eucharist? Why the sacrament of Reconciliation? Why did Jesus come? Who is he, really? What are we to believe?

We need to explain these concepts clearly to non-believers and our fellow believers alike.

But once those words start, once the teaching begins, there are potential traps which can ruin the entire process and the goal of evangelization. We must make sure our words answer the following questions, among others:

Does our belief adhere to the true nature of our God?

Does our belief help or hurt us in our personal lifelong journey with Christ toward our final salvation?

Does our belief help or hurt us in our attempt to evangelize unbelievers?

The impact of PIE upon evangelization, therefore, begins when we Christians begin to use our words. We can lead an outwardly holy life, we can speak and act with kindness and forgiveness, we can exude peace of heart in times of trouble, and we can avoid the obvious sins of the flesh that outsiders may otherwise recognize within us. But, eventually, to truly bring others to Christ, we need to speak to them about our Lord. We need to teach them the truth, in addition to being a living witness and example.

Ponder, then, how the doctrines of Predestined Individual Election come across. Sure, we can tell someone that Jesus loves them, that they have been called personally from the beginning of time to spend eternity with the other elect in heaven. We can claim there is no path to salvation beyond one single Christian belief, one specific Christian theology.

Implicit in those words, however, are the seeds of questions that will haunt potential new believers.

"What about my parents? What about my friends? They did not believe. They had never even heard about Christ."

"What about my spouse if he or she does not come to faith? What if my children follow their culture and their friends and fail to outwardly come to Jesus?"

"Are my loved ones damned to the torments of hell? And, oh dear God, if they are, then have you, Lord, foreordained their condemnation from the beginning of time! Just because you felt like it?"

And, at some point in most Christian lives, "God, at this current moment, I no longer believe, does this mean that I never truly had faith, that you never truly regenerated my soul, and you have counted me as an enemy since the beginning of time, beyond all hope?"

7.3 Communal Predestination

TULIP was an acronym that came initially from a group of Protestants who opposed Calvinistic thought. They sought a way to clearly identify their complaints with Calvinism, but the Calvinists took a list of their five points, accepted them, and reaffirmed that they represented the core of what they believed. I similarly found the shorthand 'PIE' to present a quick way to clearly identify the troubling and divisive doctrines within the Reformed church.

To contrast this line of Evangelical thought leading to Predestined Individual Election, and adhere more closely to the scriptures we have already reviewed, perhaps Communal Predestined Election (CPE) is a better description. The biblical idea seems simple. God is all-powerful and sovereign. He has a plan, which included the Incarnation, Life, Crucifixion, and Resurrection of Christ. He calls us, all of us, in various ways to respond to himself. Those who do respond, obey Jesus as Lord, and trust Christ as Savior, have joined the community of Christian believers. God predestined this community for salvation. We, those *who remain* in this community of faith, will be among the elect.

If this description reflects the *predestined* result of *election* to eternity in heaven for those living within the *community* of believers, what is not included in the idea of CPE? CPE does not claim that simply being a 'member' of an established Christian Church community is enough to save us. Jesus told the 'hypocrites' of his time who believed their membership in the Jewish race was enough that they were living as though they were among the lost.

A person might be born and baptized within the Catholic (or Protestant) church and yet live a faithless life. One can be born within a Christian community, and may even regularly attend Mass/services, and yet still choose to reject Jesus.

They, those individuals born within a visible 'community' of faith, must still make the same choices as those born outside the visible community of faith. Those who choose to continually repent, continually obey (love) Christ, continually seek a relationship with the Father and the visible family of Christ the Lord left in the world – these are members of the community of believers living within God's eternal, sovereign, and pre-destined plan for salvation. Should they persevere in this faith, they, again, will be the elect.

Chapter 8

A Cloud of Witnesses

8.1 James

When first attending Evangelical services, I knew there
was one book in the New Testament that was often cited to
oppose the sola fide (faith alone) claims of the Reformed faith.
In fact, as the Reformation developed, Martin Luther suggested this book to be removed from Christian education.

> Martin Luther was openly critical of James, and
> he wondered whether the epistle belonged in our
> Bibles, but he never formally proposed it should be
> removed. He did, however, suggest it be thrown out
> of schools:
>
> "We should throw the epistle of James out of this
> school, for it doesn't amount to much. It contains not
> a syllable about Christ. Not once does it mention
> Christ, except at the beginning."[6]

Luther's angst with the Book of James is understandable.
There is only one place in all of scripture where the phrase

'faith alone' is used, and that is in the book of James. In this one and only mention, St. James – inspired by the same Holy Spirit that inspired Paul as he wrote Romans – stated, "You see that a person is considered righteous by what they do and *not by faith alone*" (Jas. 2:24).

Now, when I began attending Evangelical services with their more literal interpretation of the scriptures, I wanted to point to James 2:24 and say, 'game over.' What we *do*, according to James, is critical. 'Faith alone' is NOT how we are considered righteous.

Could this concept be any more clearly laid out for us within God's Holy Writ? If our *deeds* are important, then where can we go with confidence to find out what those deeds should and should not be? In my mind, to the Church Jesus left behind and nursed for 2000 years through his Apostles and their followers?

But might that approach be too simple-minded, and possibly even mistaken? Perhaps we would fall into the same trap I accuse others of – taking one or a few verses out of context to create or support a specific theology.

So, I delved more deeply into James. Perhaps, I thought, if I found so much in the areas of scripture used to defend the ideas of Calvinism (as we've detailed in the previous chapters), then there would be more to be found in the Book of James that would continue to point us away from Predestined Individual Election.

The more I considered James and noticed very little of the

verbiage Paul used regarding predestination and the like, I realized this was probably because James did not face the same questions and challenges as Paul. At the very least, he was not trying to answer those difficult questions of Jew versus Gentile in this single letter. No, his target audience was his fellow Jews who had converted to Christianity.

Does this mean that James did not believe in the importance of faith? No, James spends the next few paragraphs speaking in detail about faith and perseverance in the face of current trials. Again, without a mixed audience of Jew and Gentile, he doesn't use the same phraseology as Paul, but he does reaffirm the meaning of our faith, assuring those who persevere will win the 'crown of life that the Lord has promised to those who love him.' (Jas. 1:12).

However, the theme of the entire first chapter is a clear call to those who have, in James' opinion, the *choice* to persevere (or not), to have faith (or to fall away), to blame God for their trials and temptations (or to live a life of faithfulness).

But, James is eager to say, the true believer, the true newly adopted brother or sister of Christ does not just listen, does not just express faith, they also *do*.

Do not merely listen to the word, and so deceive yourselves. Do what it says. Anyone who listens to the word but does not do what it says is like someone who looks at his face in a mirror and, after looking at himself, goes away and immediately forgets what he looks like. But whoever looks intently into the perfect law that gives freedom, and continues in it—not forgetting what they have heard, but doing it—they will be blessed in what they do. (Jas. 1:22-25)

Some criticize the Catholic church for being 'religious,' as if Jesus was critical about religion. This despite the fact that the Trinity (including Jesus) designed the Old Testament Jewish religion. For the post-Resurrection Christian, James writes that religion (properly practiced and including the care of those in need), is critical. James wrote:

Those who consider themselves religious and yet do not keep a tight rein on their tongues deceive them-selves, and their religion is worthless. *Religion that God our Father accepts* as pure and faultless is this... (Jas. 1:26-27)

Finally, Paul wrote in Romans that Abraham was con-sidered righteous by faith. For some, Paul's writings are pre-eminent, so they either ignore James or claim that his words must be interpreted differently from their plain message. For James wrote:

Was not our father Abraham considered righteous for what he did when he offered his son Isaac on the altar? You see that his faith and his actions were working together, and his faith was made complete by what he did. And the scripture was fulfilled that says, "Abraham believed God, and it was credited to him as righteousness," and he was called God's friend. You see that a person is considered righteous by what they do and not by faith alone. (Jas. 2:22-24)

Looking objectively at Genesis, we discover why these two statements about Abraham can both be true. Both writers quote Genesis 15:6, which states that Abraham's faith was credited to him as righteousness. But was Genesis 15:6 speaking about a spiritual righteousness given through regeneration and leading to eternal life?

No.

Genesis 15:6 discusses only God's choice of Abraham to be the 'father of many nations.'

James, however, continues where Paul stopped short. He continues to Genesis 22, where the Lord has demanded Abraham sacrifice his son, Isaac. The faith of Abraham, proved by his actions, confirms the truth of his faith and the choice of God to bless him with a great inheritance.

Now I know that you fear God, because you have not withheld from me your son, your only son. I swear by myself, declares the LORD, that because you have done this and have not withheld your son, your only son, I will surely bless you and make your descendants as numerous as the stars in the sky and as the sand on the seashore. (Gen. 22:12, 16-17)

No one, I believe, should use James to damage the faith of another Christian. Even if we thought the Apostle's words completely destroy key tenets of Luther and Calvin's interpretations of Christianity, I'd much rather have Evangelical Christians who are strong in faith in Jesus than ex-Evangelicals who lose their faith in Christ altogether after finding one or more of the core convictions they have been taught are wrong.

However, since in James we find portion of the New Testament so forcibly at odds with the thought of salvation through faith alone, maybe those who believe this Reformed anthem should refrain from condemning other Christ followers who have accepted the words of James as part of their understanding of the faith.

...humbly accept the word planted in you, which can save you....Do not merely listen to the word, and so deceive yourselves. *Do* what is says. (Jas. 1:10)

8.2 Feed My Sheep

I believe in the Bible, but I don't believe every part of the Bible is equally important. That doesn't mean that parts of the

Bible are not true or inspired or helpful. Those are two different issues. But, clearly, I doubt it was God's intent that we spend as much time studying the details of the Israelite tribes in the Book of Kings or Numbers as we do Jesus' Passion stories in the Gospels.

Even those who claim *sola scriptura,* there is a clear hierarchy in terms of the authors of the New Testament. For the Evangelical communities I've been a part of, all begins with Paul's Epistles, then Hebrews, Revelation and the Gospels, and finally the writings of the three non-Gospel writers who actually lived with Jesus - Peter, John and James. If you've been born into an Evangelical faith community, you may not notice that this is happening, but simply add up the number of sermons spent covering Romans, or Corinthians or Galatians, and compare that total to the sermons that cover Second Peter or First John.

In the early centuries of the faith, there was a heresy taught by Marcion who insisted that the Christian faith (and Bible) should be based upon the letters of Paul and the Gospel of Luke (the follower of Paul) alone. *Sola Paulus,* I suppose we can say, and I am afraid too many Reformed pastors and theologians walk very close to the edge of this heresy today.

Not too long ago, I listened to a question and answer session with leaders of the Reformed Church hosted by Ligonier Ministries. One questioner asked the panel members to share their favorite book of the Bible. They answered Psalms, Second Corinthians, and Romans. I was shocked that not one of these Christian leaders mentioned any of the books that 'star' Jesus. Not one of these leaders mentioned the Gospel of John, or the Gospel of Luke, or that of Matthew, or the work of Mark. It seemed very odd to me that any Christian would pick a book of the Bible as their favorite that is not one of the biographies of our Lord himself.

For a Catholic, at every single Mass throughout our lifetimes, we have a reading from one of the four Gospels, so the primary focus is always on Jesus' life. We do spend more time reading Paul's words than those of the other New Testament writers, but this is more or less in proportion to the number of his recorded writings as it is a reflection of some sort of primacy concerning his letters.

I am not saying we need to spend twice as much time studying Peter as Paul, even if I believe Peter was Jesus' hand-picked leader of his infant Church. I fully realize that Paul's ability to write made him a better tool for God to use when expounding the deeper interpretations of the faith. He must also have faced more challenging questions on his multi-nation missionary journeys than did other early Christian leaders.

At the same time, we must not deemphasize or ignore James, as we discussed above, or John, whose own travels may not have covered the geographic range of Paul but did span more of early-Christian history in terms of time. We must also not ignore the one-and-only man Jesus commanded to 'feed my sheep,' that being Peter. For Peter was the first leader of the Church upon whom the Holy Spirit physically descended as tongues of fire. He was the one entrusted both by this Spirit and the other Apostles to make the first public pronouncement of the faith, with words powerful enough to convert thousands through a single sermon. His was the 'altar-call' of all of history's great altar-calls.

So, what is it that Peter adds to our discussion of Predestined Individual Election?

One of the most direct sections in which he covers this difficult issue comes in Second Peter, chapter one, starting at verse three. He reminds us that God is the one who should be thanked for providing us what is necessary for 'life and godliness.' This should please Evangelicals who want to focus our proper worship and reliance on our all-powerful and sovereign Lord.

Then, in verse five, Peter lists traits like self-control and knowledge, that all Christians should 'make every effort to add' to their faith. He says in verse eight that if we do so, 'they will keep you from being ineffective and unproductive in your knowledge of Jesus Christ.' I don't believe that statement would be denied by any Christian no matter their stance on election.

Peter finishes his thought in the next verse, 'If anyone does not have them, he…has forgotten that he has been cleansed from his past sins.' (2 Pet. 1:9)

This verse clearly states our faith in Christ has cleansed us from our 'past' sins. That certainly would adhere more to a

Catholic outlook on justification versus the idea that faith in Christ wipes away all of our sins – past, present, and future; once for all, immediately upon our conversion.

The following verse further points us in that direction. He says in verse ten, "Therefore, my brothers and sisters, make every effort to confirm your calling and election. For if you do these things, you will never stumble" (2 Pet. 1:10). (Note, the King James Version uses the word 'fall' instead of 'stumble').

This verse, if we 'unpack it' (to use a favorite Evangelical expression), says that *if* we *do* certain things, 'you will never stumble (fall).' With that, Peter implies that Christian believers (to whom he addressed his letter) can fall. It is possible for a person who once had faith and the forgiveness of sins to still turn away. He exhorts his believing readers to continue to be eager to 'do these things,' for only then will they never stumble.

But, perhaps, the Calvinist might say, 'We can be on our predestined path individually for election, we can have faith in Christ, but still make mistakes and stumble. That does not mean that we live with the possibility of falling completely from the faith and losing our salvation.'

Peter precluded this argument in the third chapter, making it perfectly clear that belief in Jesus Christ at one moment in our lives does not guarantee salvation. We instead need to choose God and do the things he mentioned above to build and maintain our faith. To 'false prophets' within the family of believers, he wrote,

If they (believers) have escaped the corruption of the world by knowing our Lord and Savior Jesus Christ and are again entangled in it and are overcome, they are worse off at the end than they were at the beginning. (2 Pet. 2:20)

8.3 The Last Words

There are other very informative writings in the New Testament, such as 1 Corinthians, where Paul reiterates his theme that a believer's sins still matter in terms of our salvation (as we found in Galatians 5 and Ephesians 5, above):

Or do you not know that wrongdoers will not inherit the kingdom of God? Do not be deceived: Neither the sexually immoral nor idolaters nor adulterers nor men who have sex with me nor thieves nor the greedy nor drunkards nor slanderers nor swindlers will inherit the kingdom of God. (1 Cor. 6:9-10)

A review of the New Testament would not be complete, however, if we ignored the portion that attracts so much attention from today's Evangelical mind. Building upon the story told in the Book of Revelation, we witness attraction and intrigue regarding the 'end times' as portrayed in books like the Left Behind series. Specifically concerning our discussion on the topic of election, are there clues we should mine from this book of Revelation so often taken literally by Evangelicals.

In the opening chapters of Revelation, John offers details of a vision provided by his real-world good friend and eternally resurrected Lord and Savior, Christ Jesus. He addresses these chapters to seven of the local churches of his time. Churches, we can assume, either started by those who lived with Christ or the Apostles who directly taught the faith.

Calvinism, as we've discussed, claims that all individuals who lived in these Christian Churches had once been Totally Depraved prior to receiving regenerative saving grace and faith through the Holy Spirit. These people, individually, who lacked the strength to resist God-predestined fate but now professed faith in Christ, could never again be lost, for God preserves his people to the end.

With that in mind, what did John pass on to us from Jesus in this final book of the Bible?

Jesus first addresses the Church of Ephesus. To the Ephesians, spoken of only as a community and not as individuals, he offers praise, condemnation, and a warning. In the end, he says,

> Yet I hold this against you: You have forsaken the love you had at first. Consider how far you have fallen! Repent and do the things you did at first. If you do not repent, I will come to you and remove your lampstand from its place. (Rev 2:4)

Jesus tells the Ephesians that, despite choosing to repent and come to him in the first place, their new choices against the faith may cause them to be forsaken. He gives them a choice to repent or he will reject them and their church.

Next, to the church in Pergamum, Jesus says,

> You did not renounce your faith in me, not even in the days of Antipas, my faithful witness, who was put to death in your city—where Satan lives.
>
> Nevertheless, I have a few things against you: There are some among you who hold to the teaching of Balaam, who taught Balak to entice the Israelites to sin so that they ate food sacrificed to idols and committed sexual immorality. Likewise, you also have those who hold to the teaching of the Nicolaitans.
>
> Repent therefore! Otherwise, I will soon come to you and will fight against them with the sword of my mouth. (Rev 2:13-16)

We can't help but notice here key concepts from the Lord himself. First, he addresses communities and not individuals. Individual faith and the decision to repent are of course implied, but Jesus thinks about his readers primarily in terms of a community. Jesus asks those in this community of the elect to repent. If they do not repent, if they do not make the ongoing choice to come back to him in humility, what does

Jesus say will happen? He will fight against them with the sword in his mouth.

Jesus also commends the faith of those who had not fallen away, even when one of their own had been killed for the faith. But if this faith had been eternally pre-ordained by God and those who came to faith are preserved and never have the possibility of falling away, then why the commendation?

We next find a similar treatment and exhortation to the Church in Thyatira:

> I know your deeds, your love and faith, your service and perseverance, and that you are now doing more than you did at first. You tolerate that woman Jezebel, who calls herself a prophet. By her teaching she *misleads my servants* into sexual immorality and the eating of food sacrificed to idols. I have given her time to repent of her immorality, but she is unwilling. So, I will cast her on a bed of suffering, and I will make those who commit adultery with her suffer intensely, unless they repent of her ways. (Rev 2:19-23)

To this church, Jesus first praises the believers for doing more than they had done at first. However, he then levels his attack upon one particular sinner within their midst. Jezebel taught sexual immorality and other sinful behavior. But she was also, evidently, a believer and part of the church. But was she then of the elect? Jesus says he gave her time to repent and yet she has not and so she, perhaps once considered a 'saint' by others in the local church, will now face punishment. And, Jesus says, the rest of his 'servants' who follow her ways will be cast out unless they 'repent.'

Jesus ends his exhortation of the people of Thyatira through John at the end of that chapter:

> To the one who is victorious and *does my will* to the
> end, I will give authority over the nations. (Rev 2:26)

Doing Jesus' will to the end, therefore, is a call to action; it does not read here as a forgone conclusion, or a reliance only upon a feeling of faith.

Our tenuous position as believers and part of the elect communities in which we live our faith is all the more evident in the words Jesus uses when addressing the church in Sardis:

> I know your deeds; you have a reputation of being
> alive, but you are dead. Wake up! Strengthen what
> remains and is about to die, for I have found your
> *deeds* unfinished in the sight of my God. Remember,
> therefore, what you have received and heard; hold it
> fast, and *repent.* But *if* you do not wake up, I will
> come like a thief, and you will not know at what
> time I will come to you. (Rev 3:1-3)

Jesus says that whatever faith was once in this community is 'about to die.' These saints will not be preserved unless they 'hold it fast, and repent.' They need to make the choice to 'wake up.' Notice, again, the key words supporting the idea of human-will – 'deeds,' 'repent,' and, of course, '*if*'. Jesus did not consider these people to be in a state of perpetual salvation. They must properly exercise their choice to remain with him and the community of faithful followers.

Christ tells us, through these comments to the early Christian churches, to 'repent' and come back to him with faith. To do what is right. He tells us to – as he also instructed his Apostles during his earthly ministry – build and maintain our faith by asking and knocking and seeking. To make a decision, by his counsel, to buy the gold of the faith, the pure white clothing of a saint, and salve to help us to see the truth. These things are not given only through the work of regeneration provided to certain individuals. Our continual faith, this ongoing relationship within the elect Church of Christ, is a joint work between us and our Savior. Jesus tells the Church at Laodicea:

> But you do not realize that you are wretched, pitiful, poor, blind and naked. I counsel you to buy from me gold refined in the fire, so you can become rich; and white clothes to wear, so you can cover your shameful nakedness; and salve to put on your eyes, so you can see.

Those whom I love I rebuke and discipline. So be earnest and repent. Here I am! I stand at the door and knock. If *anyone hears my voice and opens the door,* I will come in and eat with that person, and they with me. (Rev 3:17-20)

Chapter 9

Romans 10-15

By exploring the scriptures, I slowly reconciled myself to the idea that Paul wrote his letter to Rome primarily to heal the Jewish/Gentile divide within the church. Romans 8 and 9, if read alone, can be interpreted to support some aspects of Predestined Individual Election but, in the broader context, the other interpretation we've discussed is far more plausible. Since other first-generation Christian leaders faced many of the same challenges, it would not be surprising to find similar themes throughout the New Testament. As we reviewed above, James, Peter, and John support the broad themes of personal freedom and true moral responsibility, along with the common call for all people to follow Christ in both faith and action. Paul agreed with these views in his other writings we touched upon, especially in Galatians and Ephesians.

But does our theory continue to make sense as we move beyond Romans 9? Does Paul continue to focus upon unifying Jews and Gentiles within the Church, or do we instead find hints of the tenants of TULIP? While Paul did not write with the idea of the current layout of our biblical chapters, the very first sentence in Romans 9 clearly reflects his concern that fellow Jews were cut off from Christ.

> For I could wish that I myself were cursed and cut off from Christ for the sake of my people, those of my own race, the people of Israel. (Rom. 9:3-4)

These sentiments are echoed by the very first sentences of what we now consider Romans 10. Paul begins the chapter writing that, "my heart's desire and prayer to God is for all Israelites to be saved" (Rom. 10:1).

He then states that he can personally testify as to how zealous and sincere his former Jewish brethren are for God, but that their 'zeal is not based on knowledge' (Rom. 10:3).

Paul's continual focus on the unity between Jew and Gentile in the Church is promoted again as he tries to convince the Jews that they can be zealous concerning not only the Old Testament law, but also concerning the faith that was also proclaimed by the Jewish prophets:

> As Scripture says, "Anyone who believes in him will never be put to shame." For there is no difference between Jew and Gentile—the same Lord is Lord of all and richly blesses all who call on him, for, "Everyone who calls on the name of the Lord will be saved." (Rom 10:11-13)

However, if we accept that his overall theme was contrasting Jew and Gentile in order to bring them together in a single faith community, Paul seems here to clearly make the point that the current generation of Israelites relied upon their adherence to the detailed rules of the Old Testament law to save them. They did not live by the 'spirit' of the Law and a personal relationship with God now available through Christ.

By the time of his writing this book to the Romans, many Gentiles accepted Christ as their Savior while many of his fellow Jews were still lost due to their denials. But the Jewish readers of this book and those Paul taught on a daily basis must have complained that they were the Chosen People, and therefore how were they now being rejected by God? They must have insisted to the Apostle, as did those who once visiting Peter (Galatians 2:12), that the Old Testament rules were still required. To many Jews, Paul's rejection of the Law, and by this the seeming rejection of *them* and their heritage, must have seemed horribly unfair.

But Paul reminds them again that this plan to bring the opportunity of salvation to the Gentiles was clearly God's plan as expressed through the Old Testament writers. They, the Jews, should now embrace this mercy with equal zeal for through these new Gentile brethren in Christ, they too will benefit. In Rom. 10:19-20, Paul writes:

Did Israel not understand? First, Moses says,
"I will make you envious by those who are not a

nation; I will make you angry by a nation that has no understanding."

And Isaiah boldly says,

"I was found by those who did not seek me;
I revealed myself to those who did not ask for me."

9.1 A Call to Family

Does Paul maintain in Romans 11 that God unfairly rejects those Jews he previously demanded so much from, and that this rejection part of some sort of eternal plan to condemn this generation of Jews individually?

Paul opened chapter 11 by asking, "Did God reject his people? By no means! I am an Israelite myself, a descendent of Abraham, from the tribe of Benjamin. God did not reject his people, whom he foreknew" (Rom. 11:1-2).

But wait. We must address the word here that very closely adheres to the ideas contained within Predestined Individual Election. The small but powerful word, 'foreknew.'

Did Paul claim here that God foreknew which of his readers *individually* be granted his love, mercy, and regeneration? Does he teach us here that others, individually, are left only capable of rejecting Christ?

Just the opposite, in fact.

Paul wrote that despite God's seeming rejection of the Jewish nation following the Resurrection of Christ, God did not in fact 'reject his people, whom he foreknew.' The fact that these people had been God's chosen ones, descended from Abraham and counted righteous through him, did not guarantee for them eternal life. In fact, most now rejected the path to heaven through Jesus. Yet, Paul reassured his Jewish readers that their rejection of Christ was not God's doing, *he* did not reject *them* (implying that *they* were the ones who rejected *him*).

Moreover, the object of Paul's word, 'foreknew,' were not individuals but the 'people' (the Jewish nation). The specific individual members of the Old Testament elect 'people' that God 'foreknew' could not have been predestined for salvation individually because many now rejected Christ. They were a foreknown Chosen People that was still being called by God individually to come back to him in faith and obedience. Paul exhorted them, those who at the moment of his writing seemed reprobate and lost, to come back to God through faith toward salvation, "Did they (the Jews) stumble so as to fall beyond recovery? Not at all!" (Rom. 11:11).

The Jews (again, God's former chosen elect) were unsaved due their *current choices* not to believe in the Risen Lord, "Rather, because of their transgression..." (Rom. 11:11).

In other words, Paul said the Jews as a nation are lost, but not in terms of every individual. To his individual Jewish readers, he wrote that they are all individually called to come to Christ. God's plan was to offer salvation to both Jew and Gentile by now pointing the Jews away from the Old Testament law and toward Christ.

Rather, because of their (Jews) transgression, salvation has come to the Gentiles to make Israel envious. But if their transgression means riches for the world (the Gentiles), how much greater riches will their full inclusion bring! (Rom 11:11-12)

How wonderful! Paul shows his Christian believers that the Gentiles as a community need the Jews, and the Jews then currently need the Gentiles. The Jews lack of faith and transgressions made it clear that salvation was not due only through the Old Testament law and therefore Gentiles had the confidence to come into the Church. Then, in turn, through envy toward the Gentiles, some Jews would also turn to accept Christ as their Savior.

The ideas of personal choice, personal freedom, and the ability we have been given as individuals to either accept or reject the call of Christ are even more directly explained as we delve more deeply into Chapter 11. Right after Paul makes references to God *hardening the hearts* of people – words that are used by those who believe in TULIP to support their view that the Reprobate are individually and irresistibly predestined by God's sovereign choice for damnation – Paul writes, "Again I ask: did they stumble so as the fall beyond recovery? Not at all!" (Rom. 11:11).

This verse alone proves that those who once could be counted outside of God's elect still have the individual choices to believe in and return to God. They are not beyond recovery. Many of the former elect community of Jews at Paul's time stumbled over the 'rock' of Christ, but the Apostle says here they did not stumble beyond the ability to recover and regain their position as part of God's new, and true, elect.

If PIE is correct and believers are saved once-for-all, the Reprobate are then lost once-for-all. But this is not true, Paul tells us. He believed that even by his writings some of the former elect would become envious of those now in the Church and come to Christ.

> In the hope that I may somehow arouse my own people to envy and save some of them. If their rejection brought reconciliation for the world, what will their acceptance be but life from the dead? (Rom. 11:14-16)

Paul did not write to those he believed God individually predestined for perpetual faith; instead, his words are those of the man who hopes some of the Jews will make the right choice through their human-will to come back to God through his Savior, even if their choices are motivated by envy through reading his letter. Think about this in light of Reformed theology. Paul seeks to generate a sinful human response – envy – in hopes of achieving a more critical goal, turning his fellow Jews toward Christ. Do we truly believe that if God predetermined the election (and faith) of only certain individuals that Paul would seek to bring about that faithful choice through our sinful desires?

Paul desired to entice beneficial choices from his Jewish readers who currently denied Christ. He also commented on the opposite end of the spectrum, warning the Gentiles who were currently Christ-followers that they must avoid the choices that could then lead to their demise. Paul considered no one, including the believing Gentiles of his day, as being once-save, always-saved.

Paul emphasized unity between his Gentiles and Jews readers. Seemingly, there were Gentiles who boasted that they had been moved into God's family after the Lord rejected some of his original Chosen People. Paul commented on this reality in the new Church, "Do not consider yourselves (the Gentiles) to be superior to those other branches (the Jews)," Rom. 11:18. Paul told the Gentiles, "You will say then, '(those) branches were broken off so I could be grafted in'" (Rom. 11:19).

Now, returning to the requirements of TULIP, the Gentiles now in the Church must have been once Totally Depraved. They, according to the Reformers, could only be in the Church Paul writes to in Rome after being regenerated with irresistibly grace by God. And, therefore, they could never fall, since they would be Preserved by the Lord.

And, yet, Paul tells the believing Gentiles,

Granted. But they were broken off *because of unbelief* and you stand by faith. Do not be arrogant but tremble. For if God did not spare the natural branches, he will not spare you either. Consider therefore the kindness and sternness of God: sternness to those who fell, but kindness to you, *provided* that you *continue* in his kindness. Otherwise you also will be cut off. And if they (the Jews) *do not persist* in unbelief they will be grafted in. (Rom. 11:20-22)

Paul is clear. The Jews (once believers and followers in God) have been cut off for unbelief in Christ, and currently believing Gentiles are warned that they too might one day fall and be cut off.

Let us consider these statements once again from our 'if/then' point of view. Paul says '*provided* you continue...' Does it make sense that he is saying in essence, 'If you find yourselves continuing in the state of belief, then you will continue to live with God'? Or do his words better reflect the idea, 'If you believe and make the right choices, then you will not be cut off'? The answer is obvious. He is urging his readers to make the choice to continue in their efforts to follow Christ as Lord and Savior?

9.2 Last Thoughts for Rome

The last four chapters of Romans are often overlooked but they do provide additional clues worth considering. In Romans 13, Paul again stresses the importance of proper actions, as he tells his readers that they are asleep and need to 'wake up'.

> The hour has already come for you to wake up from
> your slumber, because our salvation is nearer now
> than when we first believed. The night is nearly over;
> the day is almost here. So let us put aside the deeds of
> darkness and put on the armor of light. Let us behave
> decently, as in the daytime, not in carousing and
> drunkenness, not in sexual immorality and debauch-
> ery, not in dissension and jealousy. Rather, clothe
> yourselves with the Lord Jesus Christ, and do not
> think about how to gratify the desires of the flesh.
> (Rom.13:11-14)

Another interesting comment is found in Romans 14,
which seems to directly contradicts the Reformed doctrine of
the Perseverance of the Saints. The Apostle states that there
are people *for whom Christ died* who can be destroyed by their
sinful actions (here, he speaks of eating something that
another Christian believes is sinful and thus for that other
person it is sinful).

> Do not by your eating destroy someone for whom
> Christ died. (Rom. 14:15)

This statement makes two key points. First, a believer can
be spiritually 'destroyed.' This only makes sense if Paul is
speaking of someone he considers saved who is then later

destroyed. Second, Paul maintains that even these people who may end up destroyed are individuals for whom Jesus died. Thus, the atonement was not limited, at least from God's point of view. The work of Jesus on the Cross, in this verse, is limited only by the choices of those who ate what they believed was sinful.

Paul then concludes where he began, coming full circle around his theme of bringing both Jew and Gentile believers into a single family within Christ. He repeats from the opening chapter here at the end.

> For I am not ashamed of the gospel, because it has the power of God that brings salvation to everyone who believes: first to the Jew, then to the Gentile. (Rom. 1:16)
>
> For I tell you that Christ has become a servant of the Jews on behalf of God's truth, so that the promises made to the patriarchs might be confirmed and, moreover, that the Gentiles might glorify God for his mercy. (Rom. 15:8-9)

Instead of Predestined Individual Election, Paul wrote to the Romans that God, through Christ, had in this post-Resurrection time established two groups, those (former Jew or Gentile) choosing to live within the community that would eventually be called Christian; and those (former Jew or Gentile) choosing to exist within the community which rejected the Lord. To the one community, there is a pre-destined path toward salvation through Jesus. A *Communal* Predestined Election. The Christian church.

Whether his readers, as individuals, remained within this Christian faith community was up to them.

Chapter 10

Jesus Speaks

One of the things I have noticed in terms of Evangelical preaching is the over-emphasis on the New Testament writings of St. Paul. The Apostle is certainly a great inspiration to all of us, and a critical leader/missionary within the young Christian Church. He wrote a broad swath of the New Testament, but the Evangelical focus on his letters comes at the expense of other writers, especially the four authors of the biographies of Jesus. This emphasis on Paul was critical for Luther and the early Reformers who believed they found in him the basis for theologies that pointed away for the need of Catholicism.

During my experiences attending two different Evangelical churches, there has been multiple times where the pastors drilled down into one of Paul's letters in the New Testament, discussing in great detail Ephesians or Timothy or Corinthians. These preachers often proceeded through these letters verse-by-verse, attempting to decipher the true Christian faith from within a few words of Paul.

None of this is wrong except for the fact that within a

typical Evangelical service this preaching is the primary focus. By spending forty-five to fifty minutes focused on a few verses that Paul wrote to the early church limits any time and exposure that should be accorded to the life and teachings of Jesus.

This is not meant to be an attack upon Evangelicals, who of course consider all discussions of the New Testament to be inherently focused on Jesus. I recall, for example, an extended time when we studied the book of Ephesians, spending roughly six months discussing Paul's words. During this time, we heard almost nothing actually spoken or lived or taught by Jesus himself.

Contrast this to the Catholic Mass.

Every Mass focuses upon the one thing that was a main focus of all four of the Gospel writers, and mentioned multiple times throughout the New Testament. The sacrifice of Jesus Christ, his Last Supper, and the Eucharist. The Catholic Mass reminds us of Jesus's sacrifice and our need to seek personal repentance and forgiveness. We recite the words Jesus commanded us to say in prayer. We profess our faith in the Trinitarian God with the words first developed by the Church Fathers in the 300s to verify who Jesus is – God incarnate, Son of the Father.

Our Lord's words and deeds are read every single week from one of the four New Testament Gospels. The church often pulls in a reading on the same theme from the Old Testament and another from the New Testament (including the writings of Paul), but in the end they all focus back upon the Savior, Jesus Christ.

In the earlier sections of this book, I spent a lot of time focusing on the areas that seems to be at the heart of the Protestants/Evangelical theology, the sections they use as the foundation for a so-called 'systematic' theology. By finding scriptural 'proof' of what they interpreted as a predestined group of people individually set apart by God from all eternity, the earliest Protestants were able to justify their split from the mother church. Evangelicals up to this day see this part of Christian theology as dividing themselves from other Christ-followers whom they reject.

Many Evangelicals believe the main proof of their position is found in Romans 9. However, I have wondered as I sat within their churches, do they also find supportive evidence for their positions from the words of Jesus himself.

10.1 Nicodemus

One point that comes up quite often when discussing the issue of salvation is the story of Jesus' meeting with Nicodemus. The story is found in John 3 and records what happened when a leading Jewish leader met with Jesus under cover of darkness. The story is about a teacher of the Law who clearly was shaken by what he saw during the earthly ministry of an itinerant preacher from Nazareth. Other Jewish leaders are recorded elsewhere discussing what to do about the Lord and reflecting upon other supposed messiahs who had come before. Nicodemus would have known about these false saviors and how they had confused some within the Chosen People, and yet he came to Jesus already having some level of faith, or at least curiosity.

John records some of the discussion between his Master and a man he normally would have regarded with knee-shaking awe. Jesus' words are so important to the Evangelical way of thinking that their entire theology is often summarized within these few verses – where we read about the need to be 'Born Again.'

Now, all Christians, including Catholics, believe we are born again with Christ, whether it comes through infant baptism, or adult conversion; whether it is only an inward assent to the Holy Spirit, or if our rebirth also includes the physical reality of the sacraments. The difficulty really comes from a few verses in which Jesus taught his fellow Jews about the workings of the Holy Spirit. He instructs Nicodemus that, like the wind itself, the Holy Spirit moves about as he wills.

Evangelicals consider this comment as proof that it is God's Sovereign Will alone which decides whom the Holy Spirit rests upon and saves. That neither Nicodemus nor anyone else can, through their own power, move the slightest bit toward God. That it is God who has predestined some of us individually for election.

As with many stories within the Bible, what was told to Nicodemus can be interpreted as Evangelicals believe, no one denying their view should claim that it is entirely illogical. But the Calvinist view is not the only logical, or evidently reasonable, view.

I've heard over and over again the argument that, just as we had no choice in terms of our physical birth, Jesus – by saying we must be 'born again' – means we have no part either in our second, spiritual birth. But is that what Jesus meant in this text?

The first thing to realize is that we clearly do not have a complete transcript, as it were, of the discussion between Nicodemus and Jesus. In John 3:2, the Pharisee praises Jesus for the miracles he is doing, but in the very next verse Jesus takes a somewhat scolding tone to his elder and makes the somewhat incongruous comment, 'no one can see the kingdom of God unless he is born again.'

It is reasonable to assume that Nicodemus, like the other Jewish leaders, were most concerned about the earthly kingdom of God? They viewed the Messiah (Jesus, perhaps?) as being a warrior king who would turn away the Romans. But Jesus would have none of that, making it clear by his comment that the 'kingdom' he was bringing was a spiritual one.

I long believed that the older man had come at night to hide his faith in Jesus from the other Jewish leaders. But, perhaps more likely, Nicodemus had come at night to ask Jesus what many of the Pharisees might have asked themselves – was Jesus the Messiah who would throw off their

Roman shackles? Nicodemus likely arrived in the cover of darkness to hide his discussion with Jesus from the Roman authorities. He, after praising Jesus for his power, planned to ask Jesus about his plans, if he had any, to reestablish the physical kingdom of Israel. This would have been a direct threat to the Roman authorities.

This makes more sense in terms of John's positioning this story early in his Gospel since the theme at the end of John 2 seemed to be a growing excitement over Jesus due to his apparent power:

> Now while he was in Jerusalem at the Passover Festi-
> val, many people saw the signs he was performing
> and believed in his name. (Jn. 2:23)

But what about Jesus' actual words, that the Holy Spirit goes where he pleases?

I propose that John, writing this Gospel decades after the Resurrection, faced some of the same issues Paul and Peter encountered. John almost certainly faced conflicts between the Jews and Gentiles in the new Christian family. He was almost certainly questioned by the Jews as to what their role in Old Testament times meant and what their new role would be now as they followed the Messiah alongside their new Gentile brethren.

John seems to tell Nicodemus that the Spirit can go anywhere it wishes, even outside the heritage of the Jewish people. For, as he said, 'flesh gives birth to flesh, but the Spirit gives birth to spirit' (Jn. 3:6). This is all the more plausible because it repeats the theme John began in John 1. There, he tells us:

> He came to that which was his own, but his own did not receive him. Yet to all who did receive him, to those who believed in his name, he gave the right to become children of God - children born not of natural descent, nor of human decision or a husband's will, but born of God. (Jn. 1:11-13)

Jesus offered to Nicodemus the answer John reminded his contemporary critics of – God can send his spirit to anyone and make members of this new Kingdom of God out of both Jew and Gentile alike. This spiritual birth is more powerful and important than the flesh birth from 'natural decent or a husband's will.' In other words, the Jewish lineage Nicodemus relied upon was of little value in the Heavenly Kingdom Christ would soon establish.

To prove the standard by which those called by the Holy Spirit are considered part of Christ's new eternal Kingdom, John wrote this in the following verses, '*whoever believes* in him shall not perish but have eternal life....to save the *whole world* through him....*whoever believes* in him is not condemned....*whoever lives* by the truth comes into the light...' (Jn. 3:16-21).

We are all given the choice, and those who choose to 'believe' and 'live' accordingly will find eternal salvation. John did not write, 'God has given faith to certain men so that they may live by truth.' He instead tells his readers that those who first *live* by truth then come into God's light. Living implies decisions and actions, not just a state in which we find ourselves. The living, John states, comes first, and then the 'light' of faith.

This interpretation is not the only logical option, but it certainly makes enough sense to cast doubt on the interpretation that this section of John *only* reflects the concepts of Predestined Individual Election. Neither interpretation should lead any Christian to doubt their underlying faith in Jesus. Looking more broadly at this section in John's Gospel should encourage all Christians to refrain from using scripture to cause rifts between those who believe they are predestined individually for salvation and those they believe were predestined to be eternal enemies.

10.2 Pure Plagiarism

One day, as I slowly passed by Chicago's Navy Pier in rush-hour traffic, I attempted to turn on a music station and zone out after a long and tiring week. I turned instead to Relevant Radio, a Catholic station in Chicago. I did not write down the name of the priest I am about to 'borrow' from, but I believe it was a very engaging host named Father Simon.

Father Simon discussed John 3, including the verses re-volving around Nicodemus we discussed above. He passed along a series of thoughts so obvious – once I heard them – that I wish all Christians, Catholic and non-Catholic alike, were listening.

As we discussed, Evangelicals tie the idea of being 'born again' found in this chapter to their concept of predesti-nation. They promote the idea that Jesus used the concept of 'birth' to indicate our complete helplessness. We are like spiritual babies, entirely unable to do anything for ourselves. Therefore, being 'born' again means the effort is all on God's side.

But, Father Simon reminded me and his other listeners that early Friday evening, the emphasis in this passage is not that we are *helpless* babies, but that we are babies, born again by the Holy Spirit as children in the faith. This radio host noted that we all are aware of several common traits among babies. Not only do they all cry, not only do they at times smell bad, and not only do they all keep us up at night.

They also…every single one of them who are healthy… grow.

So, if Jesus was saying we needed to be 'born' of the Spirit, and we want to take that statement to imply that early in our faith lives we are like babies, then Jesus is telling us we need to also *grow* in the Spirit. We are called by God to eventually become much more than helpless babies.

Paul tells his readers they were first, upon their conversions, fed baby-food and needed to grow into the adult food of the faith (1 Cor 3:2). Peter and John wrote their letters to people already Christian, and called their readers to additional reflection, action, and growth. After the resurrection, Jesus told Peter he was not to only tell the world about his Gospel, but Peter was to 'feed' his sheep, helping those born-again babies in the faith to grow.

Essentially, this priest on the radio said, the born-again baby fails if he or she does not grow. If they are not cared for and nurtured, if they do not learn and make the correct decisions and agree to care for and nurture themselves spiritually, spiritual babies will die.

Salvation does not come from simply being 'born' again. To really take this analogy of being a spiritual baby seriously, this wise priest said, we must recognize that we can be 'still-born' in the faith.

10.3 Lamps Light Our Way

We will later discuss some of the parables Jesus told, including the one about the wedding attendants who either had, or didn't have, enough oil for their lamps. Without spoiling the surprise, I think there is another part of Jesus' meeting with Nicodemus that is both critical and overlooked. I decided to put this discussion in the current section of this book because, I figure, all of my plagiarisms should be restricted to one area. The difficulty with discussing anything concerning a global, two-thousand-year-old faith is that there is very little new to say. The best we can hope to do is rephrase what other giants in the faith have said before us, or synthesize various teachings so as to answer new questions or challenges that arise as our world changes.

That said, in a moment of certain divine intervention as I was writing this section, I watched a video from another Christian apologist. He also spoke about John 3 and the idea of being 'born again.' He called attention to the fact that Jesus specifically tells Nicodemus what is required:

> Very truly I tell you, no one can enter the kingdom of God unless they are born of water and the Spirit. (Jn. 3:5)

It is a recurring theme throughout the New and Old Testament that God moves through both water and Spirit, whether it be in Genesis when the Spirit moved about the waters, or in Exodus when the Spirit lead the fleeing Hebrew nation through the sea, or when the Spirit descended like a dove upon Christ when our Lord was baptized in the waters of the Jordan.

But I wonder if there is another point being made here in John 3. Let us put ourselves in the place of the Apostle John for a moment. He wrote his Gospel to members of a Church now several decades old. A Church that by all accounts already employed some of the sacraments. We have explicit

New Testament references to baptism, the Eucharist, the priesthood, etc.

I wonder if John, in choosing which parts of his Lord's discussion with Nicodemus to include in his Gospel, specifically pointed out 'water and the spirit' to signify two of the sacraments then used by himself and the church he helped build – water baptism and confirmation through the laying on of hands. If so, might John have emphasized for his readers that they are to make the proper human-will choices to engage in the activities and sacraments of the faith community designed by God?

10.4 What Must I Do?

Learning from my Evangelical experiences, I find myself studying smaller chunks of the biblical stories in greater detail. As I reread the gospels, one story about Jesus and his interaction with those who came to him is especially intriguing and enlightening. That story reflects the questions and answers, the give and take, between the Lord and what some call the 'Rich Young Ruler.'

We all recall the story. A wealthy young man comes to Jesus and asks the ultimate question, "What must I do to inherit eternal life?" (Lk. 18:18). If we are ever going to really look at what Jesus considered to be the Gospel, the Good News of eternal life, then should we not start (and end?) right here?

Jesus first points toward obedience of the commandments, and the man responds that he has followed them all.
Jesus says there is then one thing more, 'Sell all you have and
give to the poor and...come, follow me.' The man leaves,
saddened. Jesus warns those near to him that it is easier for a
camel to pass through the eye of a needle than for the rich to
make it to heaven. His followers are amazed, 'If even the
rich...'.

Jesus says to them, (I am sure with a wink and a smile)
'What is impossible with men is possible with God' (Lk.
18:27).

I've heard, both from Catholics and Protestants, dozens
of sermons reflecting on this exchange. Some preachers aim
to reassure the wealthy of our day that they are not
automatically doomed. I've even heard one pastor insist that
the 'needle' was actually just the name of a small gate in the
walls of Jerusalem. Hard, but not impossible, for a camel to
pass through. Perhaps true, but seemingly incongruous verses
the listeners' amazement over Jesus' assertion.

After being exposed to Calvinistic thought, however,
other insights stand out concerning Jesus' interaction with
this man.

First, when asked directly what is needed for salvation,
Jesus doesn't say, 'Have faith in me.'

He first says *do* this and *do* that – and *follow* the commandments.

Second, when the young man says he has followed the

commandments, Jesus only then instructs him, '*Sell* all you have (another '*do*') and follow me," which is a combination of both faith and works, or works leading to and demonstrating faith.

What Jesus did not say in answer to the direct query regarding the path to eternal life, is 'Nothing.'

He does not say, 'You don't have to do anything, you are either part of the elect or you are not. My Father has already planned to save you from the beginning of the world, or he never will. If you discover one day that you have faith, follow me. If you don't, then even what I tell you now will have no effect upon your destiny; you will never believe me.'

I have lately come to believe this story also shows us something else just as important with regard to the theme of this book. For, if Calvinism is correct, what we must see here is a young man who was Totally Depraved. He was *dead* in sin. Even if he did follow all of God's commandments, they would say, it must have been only for social status, or greed, or something other than any desire to seek and follow God. We know this man was not part of the elect; he had not been regenerated because he later left Jesus and therefore was obviously not predestined for faith.

If so, then how did he come to Jesus in the first place?

It dawned on me that this young man, if Calvin is correct, must have been given just a *touch* of the Holy Spirit. Just enough to overcome his Total Depravity and bring him before the Lord. But then, for no reason due to the young man but only because of God's eternal Will, the Father told the Spirit, 'Never mind, we don't want him. Let us take away what we began to give him.'

God, we are told by those of the Reformed faith, is also unchanging, his ways are eternal, and he is omniscient so there is nothing this young man could have done after the first injection of the Holy Spirit that would then cause the Spirit to flee. This young man represents, in fact, every single 'back-slider' who ever went to church and looked and spoke and acted like a Christ-follower for a while, and then left the faith. Evangelicals might protest that this man never *really* had faith in the first place. But, if so, is he not the silver-tipped arrow that hits the heart of the TULIP. For there is nothing that separates him from the real-life army of people who believe at one moment in their lives that they do believe and have benefitted from Predestined Individual Election, only to fall again.

Maybe this issue should not be generalized from the example of this one man alone. Perhaps he was brought into Jesus' life for one moment only, through the omnipotence of the Father, to prove a single point for future generations. Maybe he was remembered by three of the Gospel writers only to stress the difficulty of comingling faith and riches.

But then we read about a similar situation in John Chapter 6. Jesus here tells the crowds:

> But here is the bread that comes down from
> heaven, which anyone may eat and not die. I am the
> living bread that came down from heaven. Whoever
> eats this bread will live forever. This bread is my
> flesh, which I will give for the life of the world. (Jn.
> 6:50-51)

These verses, of course, are where Catholics find powerful proof concerning the Real Presence in the Bread and Wine. But I wonder, can we find even more clues regarding our path to salvation within that chapter?

Just as with the rich young man, the account given in John 6 concerns people who had followed Christ, but then left Jesus after hearing him claim they had to eat his flesh and drink his blood. Their passionate and negative responses to his claim, perhaps, was proof positive that they understood that the Lord was talking about his *real* body and blood. But, in the context of this book, what is more telling is that these '*disciples*' actually *left* the Lord and did not return.

> From this time many of his disciples turned back and
> no longer followed him. (Jn. 6:66)

Now, these were not people who entered our Lord's presence for a brief moment. They were not faceless people in the crowd. We are told they were some of his closest followers. The word used for them in John 6 is 'disciples.' After this encounter, the Twelve remained, but likely out of those called *disciples* were some of the seventy-two enthusiastic followers elsewhere sent out by Jesus to spread the Gospel (see Luke 10).

If Reformed theology is correct, these 'disciples' must have been Jews regenerated to saving faith individually by the Holy Spirit; otherwise, they could not have believed in the Lord. But, if regenerate, they then could not have then fallen from the faith and left Jesus (just as the rich young ruler could not have come to Jesus and then left). But, they *did* fall away.

In the face of these real-life examples, TULIP wilts and dies. For either these disciples were not Totally Depraved and came to Jesus at least partially through their own choice. Or, they were Totally Depraved, and then regenerated, but the regenerative grace was not irresistible. Or, they were Totally Depraved, regenerated with Irresistible Grace, but then these 'saints' were not preserved until the end. There is simply no way to explain the falling away of the 'disciples' in John 6 in a way that is consistent with all of the Five Points of TULIP.

Instead, the biblical record here is of people who sincerely desired Jesus, followed him and became his disciples, but then made the choice to leave him due to teachings they could not reconcile within their own minds. People very much like all the rest of us – called, but responsible for their own choices and often doomed by their own failures and turning away.

10.5 The High Priestly Prayer

Out of the four Gospels, the section Evangelicals often point to is found only in John, in the portion of the book often referred to as the 'high priestly prayer' or sometimes the 'upper room discourse.' While it may be considered some-what ironic that such emphasis is placed upon John's account of the Last Supper while ignoring the other three Gospels (which detail how Jesus gave us at the same time himself in the Bread and Wine of the New Covenant), the Evangelical interpretations of Jesus' words have led to divisions within the faithful.

A key section is found in John 17, where Jesus says:

> I have revealed you (Father) to those whom you gave me out of this world. They were yours, you gave them to me and they have obeyed your word. Now they know that everything you have given me comes from you. For I gave them the words you gave me and they accepted them. (Jn. 17:6)

This paragraph, taken out of context, is often applied universally with a view that all who believe the 'correct' set of doctrines are part of the 'those,' selectively chosen to belong to the Father ('they were yours'). The Father then called some of us individually from all eternity to be given to Christ with regenerative souls which accept Jesus' words and salvation.

Jumping ahead a couple of verses, the 'exclusivity' of God's call is further witnessed by these words in which Evangelicals support the idea that Jesus does not love all people, for he only prays for some and not for the whole world:

I pray for them. I am not praying for the whole world,
but for those you have given me. (Jn. 17:9)

Now, because Evangelicals tend to study the Bible more than some lay Catholics, when Catholics hear an argument like this, I believe (from personal experience as much as anything else) our tendency is to shy away from the discussion altogether, with the assumption the Evangelical must know what they are talking about. I personally lived with this assumption for a long time, especially when faced with the challenges of these specific quotes from Jesus' pre-crucifixion prayer.

However, a careful reading of these words in the broader context of John's account enables us to see that it is almost certain that Jesus was not speaking of a universal and timeless reality applied to all individuals human beings throughout history. His words in this paragraph do not apply to everyone, but only to the apostles who were in the room with him at that Last Supper. As St. Augustine wrote concerning these verses:

"Yet we are impelled the more to understand Him as

uttering them only of those who were at that time His disciples, by what He says shortly afterwards: "While I was with them, I kept them in Thy name: those that Thou gavest me I have kept, and none of them is lost, but the son of perdition; that the Scripture might be fulfilled" (ver. 12); meaning Judas, who betrayed Him, for He was the only one of the apostolic twelve that perished."[7] (Tractate CVI)

Jesus, therefore, spoke only about the Twelve (eleven, without Judas) being given to him by the Father, and not a future community of individuals predestined for election. He thanked the Father for Peter, and Andrew, and James and John, and the rest; thanked him for granting that they had believed in him and his word; and asked the Father to protect them from the dangers and doubts that were to come.

Holy Father, protect them by the power of your name
- the name you gave me - so that they may be one as
we are one. While I was with them, I protected them
and kept them safe by the name he gave me. (Jn.
17:11-12)

At the moment these words were spoken, Jesus and his Apostles were only one week removed from the moment when the people welcomed the Lord triumphantly into Jerusalem. These people, to be consistent with Evangelical doctrine, must have then been individually predestined for salvation at that moment, for they had obviously escaped their Total Depravity due to the work of the Holy Spirit and expressed faith in Christ.

But now, after the Passover meal, Jesus knew most of these same people (who by then had lost their faith in him) would soon demand his crucifixion. Jesus was then led to openly pray before the Apostles for their own protection from both the Romans and their fellow Jews. How can we interpret his prayer to mean everyone who believes in Jesus will never be harmed when we all see around us a certain percentage of Christians who at some point in their lives fall away? His words during this High Priestly Prayer only make sense if the group he is praying about is not all followers throughout time but only the eleven faithful Apostles who had lived with him the past couple of years and shared his Last Supper with him. Their safety was a priority for the Lord. Even at the start of his Passion, Jesus says to those who capture him at Gethsemane, "I told you that I am he. If you are looking for me, then let *these* men go" (Jn. 18:8).

It appears to make much more sense to consider that John, frightened and terrified the night before the crucifixion, remembered back with amazement that he and his fellow Apostles (except, of course, Judas) were preserved safely by the Father through that fateful night and the subsequent early years of the Christian faith.

He and his companions expected death that night and

they were still hidden behind locked doors on Easter morning. Yet, right in the heart of Jerusalem, they remained safe. John wrote his Gospel to a Church reeling under persecution. He shared with his readers his memory of Jesus praying for him during that impossible time. The Father listened to those prayers of his Son and saved him, Peter, James, and the rest. John reassured his contemporary readers that Christ was certainly who he and the other Christian leaders claimed him to be. The Word of God, with the power to protect.

Instead of reading into the High Priestly Prayer a universal truth that anyone who becomes Christian does so only because God the Father decided to give Jesus that soul from the beginning of time, it would make more sense to believe John and the others – the eleven men who lived with God Incarnate! – could not explain their survival in any other terms. Instead of reading into Jesus words the concept that he was praying at the Last Supper for only a few future individuals, and that the Father in love for his Son will protect those few even from the possibility of falling away, this upper room discourse reflects John's recollection about how Jesus prayed specifically for him and the other ten. He recalled with awe and thankfulness how the Father, against all odds, kept them safe that first Good Friday.

One obvious question John was asked to answer would likely have been, 'You faced the persecution of the Jews in Jerusalem when Jesus was executed. You were in the garden with Jesus the night when the guards came to arrest him. It was just you and Peter and James with the Lord against the soldiers. How did the three of you escape unhurt? How did you stand at the foot of the Cross the next day in front of the Jewish leaders and Roman guards - and avoid arrest? How, when you faced such terrible enemies against the Church, did God protect you during those first days before that first Easter?'

Jesus prayed to his Father for the disciples' protection during that momentous occasion, prayers meant to reassure the Apostles, prayers retold by John to reassure his contemporaries. This does not mean the Father is deaf to Christ's prayer for us in the world today. He continues to protect us as he did those early disciples. However, Christ's prayer in the upper room was meant to reflect the physical and spiritual protection of his Apostles. We should not read these words to mean the spiritual protection of only a specific group of followers throughout the ages, or God's predestining each of us individually to our fates.

10.6 John 15

The 'high priestly prayer' also provides decisive insights regarding our relationship with the Lord. In John 15, he tells his Apostles that they must remain in him, and if they do not, the Father will cut them off:

> He cuts off every branch in me that bears no
> fruit, while every branch that does bear fruit he
> prunes so that it will be even more fruitful (Jn. 15:2)
>> If you do not remain in me, you are like a branch
> that is thrown away and withers; such branches are
> picked up, thrown into the fire and burned. (Jn. 15:6)

Jesus then tells them about their love for him, and his love for them. All revolving around the obedience they show and the good that they do. We see again, the great word of decision and choice – the great 'IF'. For we are called to obedience and must choose accordingly.

> As the Father has loved me, so have I loved you. Now
> remain in my love. *If* you keep my commands, you
> will remain in my love, just as I have kept my Father's
> commands and remain in his love. (Jn. 15:9-10)

As we discussed regarding John 17, the Lord can be understood here as speaking to, and about, his Apostles. And yet, does that not make the point all the more certain? Even the Apostles, given their special roles and insights, are told that they are to obey Jesus' commands, for through this is shown their love. If they so obey, they will remain in Jesus' love. If they do not, even they will be cut off and thrown away. Even they, the Apostles, were not once-saved, always-saved. Even they enjoyed the freedom to truly love the Lord.

Chapter 11

The Parables of Calvin

I fear we are about to speak roughly again about our friend Calvin. I don't intend to pile on, but let us use his name here once again as many today remember it, as synonymous with the ideas we identified as Predestined Individual Election.

Jesus' preferred method of teaching the crowds was through the use of parables. He once explained that he taught in parables so, 'he who has ears to hear, let him hear' (Lk. 8:8).

Evangelicals imply from these words that Jesus used the parables to teach only those who had been previously elected for salvation. For the rest – those eternally and personally predestined for hell – they believe the parables were purposefully used to mislead. God himself would make the meaning of the parables unintelligible.

I propose instead that what Jesus meant with his words, 'those with ears...,' is that those who make the choice to *pay attention* and *listen carefully* to his words and reflect upon their meanings would understand and benefit. Similar to what we say today when we as teachers or parents describe to our pupils and children the difference between merely hearing and truly listening to someone else.

A professor can post his class notes on-line for all to read, but it is only the student(s) who takes their class seriously and show up to listen during the lectures that gains a complete understanding of the material. The good professor, however, does not purposefully post lecture notes in a foreign language to make sure only those who knew that language would succeed.

More so, Jesus was building a Church, his Body which will grow after the Resurrection. He certainly would not have wanted any but his Apostles to later teach with authority the depths of the Christian faith. He didn't want people who simply sat down on a hillside one day and listened to him in passing to then go out to teach what they believed were universal truths about the Kingdom of God.

Let us then review a few of his most well-known parables and see what the Lord taught us regarding the Calvinist theology of Predestined Individual Election. On occasion, we will simply look at the scriptures as they were written. Other times, we may consider what the Calvinist Bible (2.0) would have said had TULIP reflected the meaning of Jesus' words.

11.1 Abraham's Bosom

As we dip our toes into this subject, it would be safest to look first at the most 'unrealistic' parable of Jesus. Most parables used by the Lord centered on the types of people that were real to his listeners; shepherds, fishermen, farmers, and even Samaritans. But in one parable, Jesus spoke about Abraham, and while Abraham was a real, historic figure, Jesus fictionalized him in his parable. In other words, Jesus didn't say, 'Just as Abraham did on Mount so and so on the fifth of a certain month...," referring to the patriarch's real actions in a real place with real historical circumstances. He instead tells a story of Abraham having a discussion outside heaven with a rich man who despised the beggar, Lazarus. Instead of rooting this parable in history, as Christ did in other references to Moses or David or Solomon, this one parable almost feels like a conversation between the fictional gods of Olympus.

This is clearly one of the most obvious parables of Jesus with a Calvinist bent. After both the beggar and the rich man die, Lazarus is taken to heaven while the greedy and spiteful rich man is cast into hell. The rich man calls out to Abraham, who is comforting Lazarus, and asks the father of the Jewish faith to send the beggar back to his like-minded brothers to warn them.

Abraham responds to the man, 'My son, if God has determined your brothers are not part of the elect, just as he had predetermined this fate for you, there is nothing you or I can say or do to save them. Even should you go back to warn them, it won't matter, they are incapable of changing their minds due to the totally depraved souls they were born with."

But...as I read the parable, Abraham did not actually say

that. Instead, the parable clearly implies that the wealthy man's brothers have had the choice to listen to the previous prophets and word of God, but they have *chosen* to not obey. Jesus stresses through Abraham's words to the formally rich man that even if faced with more dramatic proof, such as someone coming back from the dead, his brothers still will choose not to believe. They would not, in Abraham's words, 'listen,' nor would they repent. The brothers' choices condemned them, not the state into which their souls had been born.

11.2 The Prodigal Son

Now that we looked at a parable told by Jesus using the context of heaven, let us take a look at the parable that seems to have made the most impact throughout the past two thousand years – that of the Prodigal Son. A parable rooted deeply in the real-world experiences of real-world family relationships.

We've all heard this parable dissected from the point of view of the father, the point of view of the prodigal son, and the point of view of the older brother. I have heard a hundred sermons at least pointing out the many layers of meaning within this short story. If Jesus' answer to 'Give unto Caesar what is Caesar's and unto God what is God's' is the perfect example of his wisdom, then this parable the perfect example of a perfect story. For we can all see ourselves, if we are honest, in all three characters. As the prodigal who rebels, as the brother who is jealous, as the father who worries, loves, and forgives.

The only person whose point of view I've not heard preached about with relation to this parable is Calvin. If Jesus wanted to reflect the ideas of Predestined Individual Election in any of his parables, which could be better than that of the Prodigal Son. It's always dangerous to read too much meaning into any single story, of course, for Jesus seemed to always have one major point to make to his audience. For us to twist and turn his words to stretch them into virtually any possible meaning can be a dangerous and misleading game.

But, in this case, I believe the message is very clear. What does Christ teach us about our role, and the father's role, in our salvation?

First, we have a prodigal son who rebels against his father and goes to a far-off country, wasting his inheritance. Right in line with our Five Points of Calvinism, this son could be seen as being Totally Depraved. He appears lost – entirely dead in his sin. Incapable and unwilling to make even the slightest move back toward his father.

And then we find God, clearly represented in this parable by the father. He – through his powerful sovereignty – has mercy on this lost lad, sends his men to the foreign land where the boy feeds the pigs, and they pick him up out of the slop. This 'grace' the father provides this boy is irresistible and his men bring him kicking and screaming back to his home.

There, they place a white robe on the still angry and proud son, and he is kept forever within his father's home.

Of course, when I reread the story of the Prodigal Son in the Bible, I find something quite different. The 'Prodigal Son' may very well have come down to us these past two thousand years better known as the parable of the 'Repentant Son.' For in Jesus' telling, this young man found himself one day in the pig slop, and it was then and there that *he made a decision*. He made a fateful *choice*.

Whether this choice reflected a purely noble feeling or simply that he was hungry, the boy remembered his father and longed to be back home. He made a decision through his human-will to make the first faltering and shoeless steps toward safety. He hoped and trusted that, just perhaps, his father would have mercy on him. And, though his exterior was covered by rags and sores and dirt, his soul inside was no longer that of impudent child who earlier demanded his portion of his father's wealth. The first small step back home turned into a marathon of humility and the once proud and rebellious son returned in proper relation to his father, begging for forgiveness.

And the father? The boy's 'God'?

He, like our Father in heaven, was constantly watching, constantly hoping, constantly willing to receive his son back within the family. But, the Father remained at home. The Father waited. If the son would return, it would not be forced. The child would receive forgiveness, but only if that was sought through repentance. The young son who – it can be assumed – remained forever after in his father's home, had to first make a choice.

But, Jesus also knew the hearts of those who would hear him tell this parable. He knew that his Jewish brothers, especially their leaders, would be scandalized by the father's willingness to provide mercy. Thus, we also find here the character of the older brother. The one who believed he deserved to be loved, to be the sole 'elect' of his father. Who believed he had earned what his younger brother should have justly lost forever.

Just as the Jews in Paul's time thought they had earned what the Gentile Christians in the church had not, the older brother was given the answer to his prideful anger – a resounding 'no' from the Lord. A reality Paul later mimicked when he addressed the Jewish Christians in Rome who shared the exclusive demands for justice with the older brother.

11.3   The Wedding Feast

There are other parables and teachings from Jesus which are not at all compatible with Calvinism, so before we get back to the other Calvinist parables, let's discuss at least one in this group. The parable of interest here is found in Matthew 22 and takes up roughly half the chapter. It is often called the Parable of the Wedding Feast.

Here, Jesus compares the Kingdom of Heaven with a

wedding feast held by a King. This parable must have been very close to Jesus' own heart, and I would imagine he told and retold it many times for his listeners, for as he says, the King (the Father) has prepared this banquet 'for his son.'

For *him.*

When the banquet is fully prepared, the King sends his servants out to call his guests to the feast. 'But they paid no attention'…and even 'seized his servants, mistreated them and killed them' (Mt. 22:5-6).

Certainly, Jesus looked at his Jewish listeners while telling this parable, cocked his head, raised an eyebrow, and let the words sink in with the descendants of those who killed many of the Old Testament prophets. Those who would, eventually, kill *him.*

Then, the King in the parable said to his servants, 'Those I invited did not deserve to come, so go to the street corners and invite to the banquet anyone you find' (Mt. 22:9).

Here, we certainly get from Jesus' lips justification for the Christian religion to go forth to preach to the Jews and Gentiles alike, and Matthew makes a point to recall these words in his Gospel since, as we've discussed elsewhere, this issue of mixing these former Old Testament enemies faced all of the early Church leaders around the time of John's writing.

In the King's command, we also see that the saving call and initial graces of God have been offered to all and the atonement of Christ (our entry into the feast) is not limited, at least from God's point of view. It is instead restricted by us and our poor choices, for some who were invited did not in the end deserve to come, since they rejected the call.

So, even though the invite goes out to all people, and not just a limited elect who were initially invited to the Feast, Jesus makes the further point that we still need to make the correct decision and do our part. We read first about the initial plan of the King to call an original group of people who would be considered the elect, but the elect had turned him down. They were then lost.

We also read about an individual man within the new elect (those invited to the new Christian family) who, even though he heard and responded positively to the call and entered the feast, refused to wear the proper wedding clothes. Perhaps Jesus was warning the Gentiles and Jews who would one day choose to enter the second 'elect' community of the Christian faith to beware of their pride and disobedience and know that even if they at one point claim Christ their Savior, they still need to 'work out (their) salvation with fear and trembling…" (Ph. 2:12).

'For,' Jesus ends his parable, 'many are invited, but few are chosen' (Mt. 22:14).

We discover in the Parable of the Wedding Feast God's universal call, a universal offer through Christ, and proof again that a one-time profession of Christ does not guarantee immunity against a future fall.

11.4   Matthew 25

Getting back to Calvin, we have in Matthew Chapter 25 a pair of famous parables recollected together to make clear to us some of the points Jesus repeatedly made during his earthly ministry. The first parable is about ten virgins attending a wedding celebration, and the second story is told about a ruler leaving for a trip and assigning his staff, essentially, with various assets to work with during his absence.

Jesus first tells the story of ten attendants at a wedding, all of whom have brought their lamps to light the way for the groom. The groom is delayed and five of the attendants have enough oil to last through the wait while the others prepared improperly and don't have enough oil. When the groom arrives, these five who lacked oil were away trying to buy more fuel for their lamps. When they returned, they were locked out of the wedding altogether.

As we did with the previous parables, I can rephrase the story as Christ would have told it had Jesus' point been to teach us about Predestined Individual Election, but we have probably already recognized the point of this parable fairly. There were ten wedding attendants who evidently all knew the groom (were all 'believers'), but half of them later lost their salvation (acceptance into the wedding) because of their poor choices. They did not suddenly turn on the groom and hate him. They even wanted to serve him and enter the wedding party. They simply failed to *do* what was expected.

11.5 The Oil

We can try to read other truths into this parable, as we can with just about any of Christ's stories. There is a danger in doing so, of course, for we all know as parents when we tell our kids a story to make a single point, they're likely to understand a different message altogether. But I would like to at least throw this thought out for consideration.

Matthew, in the case of this story about the wedding attendants, remembered the words of Jesus and reflected upon what he, writing decades later, knew fit best within the formation and growth of the new Christian Church. In other words, at the point of writing the Gospel as a leader in Christ's Church, Matthew faced not only the task of relating to the next generation who Jesus was, but also describing and defending to his readers *why the church did the things that it did.*

Again, it is just speculation, but as I read this parable I am stuck by the focus on the oil. I wonder why Christ made the oil a central point in this story, for we have other stories about the King's feast (i.e. heaven) where the garment worn (or not worn) by the guests was a central item of concern. Why then did Jesus speak here about the oil? Why did Matthew, out of his vast memories of Jesus' sayings and, supposedly, already in possession some of the other New Testament accounts, choose to record this parable as he did? Why was not the main issue, again, that five of the attendants wore the correct wedding clothes and the other half did not (for that would provide additional internal consistency with the other Gospel accounts). Or, that five of the attendants grew tired and fell asleep, or decided other items in their lives needed to be taken care of, or simply forgot their wedding gifts?

What if Matthew assumed Jesus was here speaking about heaven and our path to ultimate salvation? That the ten wedding attendants represent us? That there may be ten of us professing faith in God and his Christ at one point in our lives but that, as he must have experienced in the real church in which he lived, many of the initial believers did not persevere in the faith and fell away by the end.

What's more, what if the primary thing he had in mind was the final coming of Christ? Not in a global sense, but at the end of our individual lives? Would we be properly prepared at that moment? Or would many of us be like these attendants about whom Jesus spoke, unprepared when our personal 'end times' comes?

And how are we to be prepared for our final moment of truth with our Lord? Again, Jesus in the parable doesn't refer to the five unwise attendants as being unbelievers or losing their God-enforced salvific faith in him (the groom), he simply says they were unprepared, and thereby ultimately lost.

So, again, why the oil? Why is Jesus using the oil as a representation of being properly prepared for his coming? Why did Matthew see this as an item of deep importance and worthy of passing on to his readers?

I propose that Jesus did in fact use this parable and he did in fact mention the oil. After the Resurrection, the Apostles reflected upon what Christ taught and (led by Holy Spirit) interpreted this parable as being a direct discussion (and warning) about how we are to maintain our preparedness to meet Christ upon our deaths. The early church leaders followed Christ's teaching and used oil as part of the prayers for those who were sick so they might receive the benefits awarded to the wise wedding attendants. They anointed the sick with holy oil and reaffirmed in those difficult (and potentially final) moments of life the person's belief and trust in the saving power of Christ. We read in James:

> Is anyone among you sick? Let them call the elders of
> the church to pray over them and anoint them
> with **oil** in the name of the Lord. (Jas. 5:14)

Matthew, having to explain to his readers why that particular ceremony was celebrated in the Church, and why it was performed as it was, focused upon the parable the disciples remembered from among Jesus' teachings prior to the Cross and Resurrection.

In other words, I believe Jesus did present this particular parable and when his disciples built the Church, they used these words to instruct them on how to prepare the sick and, we can assume, the dying to reach their eternal reward. They remembered Christ's emphasis on the oil, and therefore anointed with oil as a physical sign and symbol of their belief in Christ. Then, as the Church grew and newer Christians asked about the genesis and meaning of this ceremony, Matthew made sure this specific parable was recorded in his Gospel.

11.6   The Talents

Another parable of interest begins at Matthew 25:14 and concerns a master with his three servants. If the master loosely represents God in Jesus' story, Calvinists must then assume all three of the 'servants' are part of the elect, for they are all entrusted by the master with portions of his property (talents). This property – like the missing coin or the pearl of great value in Jesus' other examples – represents the gospel. At the beginning of this parable, then, these servants are granted a share of faith by the master.

But when the master in the parable returns from a long trip, he finds that his servants have treated the talents he graciously gave them in different ways. Two of the men worked hard, nurtured what had been entrusted to them, and like those where the seed found good soil (see below), their work produced a solid return. But the third servant who was given a share of the master's property did nothing with what he was granted. He had been part of the elect, had been at one point 'born again' as a servant of the master, but he had been essentially still-born in the faith. It was not the case that this man stole the master's money, nor even that he lost it. He protected what was given to him, he (in Calvinist terminology) 'preserved' the master's property. But that was not enough.

And what was the master's reaction to this man's lack of progress with his property? How did he treat this servant who knew what was right but decided to not obey? We read some of the most scathing remarks Jesus spoke about anyone – 'You wicked, lazy servant' (Mt. 25:26). And for the follower of TULIP who suggests that this servant is simply punished but doesn't lose his relationship with the master (his salvation with God), Jesus assures us otherwise. The master tells his other servants, "Throw that worthless servant outside, into the darkness..." (Mt. 25:30).

Just in case Matthew's readers were still unclear about the Lord's theme, his very next parable, beginning in Matthew 25:31, confirms the importance of making the right choices throughout our lives. Not just avoiding sin (as we are warned about by Paul in Galatians 5, Ephesians 5, etc.) but in proactively doing good. Jesus tells us about his return in glory and the judgment of the world. There will be those not necessarily sure of their standing with the Lord who will be saved. But not through *faith* alone in Christ. Instead, he rewards these 'sheep' due to their kind treatment of the least of their brothers and sisters in this world.

But, what about faith? What about the Reformed doctrine

that Jesus predestined anyone who claims faith in him to individually receive regeneration, and from that faith they can never fall? Jesus doesn't say that faith is worthless in this story, does he?

Not at all. But Jesus commands the 'goats' – those who rejected help for those less fortunate – to be cast into the eternal fire. But, they beg, 'Lord, when did we see you hungry...,' for they have had, or at least at this last moment, clung onto some level of faith in him, but to no avail. They knew and accepted that Jesus was 'Lord.'

11.7 Boasting

In Chapter 3, we dealt with the issue of The Fall. It was not until I understood the Evangelical outlook on this foundational point of theology that what initially seemed so obviously illogical in their chain of reasoning became at least understandable. In that case, the issue had been Total Depravity, and the doctrines that emanate from the view that we are all born by nature spiritually 'dead' due to Adam and Eve's sin. While I believe we now realize that the biblical view does not support such a radical notion of human corruption, when we take Total Depravity as our starting point we can follow mistaken, but logical and sincere, spiritual paths.

It is enlightening for all of us Christ-followers to look at one such path which leads us to a discussion about spiritually 'boasting.' In section 3.3, we discussed the analogy of God being a governor who occasionally provides a pardon for a person already, justly, sentenced to death row. A second analogy concerned the process of our salvation, and suggested we are all unable to swim and are lost far out at sea.

Some Christians, the Reformers charge, believe that as we sink below the waves, Jesus throws us a life preserver. We can be saved – we can receive the grace of the life preserver – but we must make at least some effort and grab onto the life preserver.

Reformed doctrines of TULIP are contrary to this. We, being Totally Depraved, are dead, already drowned, fish food dissolving at the bottom of the ocean. But then God, through his sovereign choice and Irresistible Grace, reaches under the water, lifts us up to the bright sunny day and resuscitates us.

Now, the question in my mind is the same as it was for many in history who bristled at these Calvinist ideas. If God alone pulls our carcasses out of the waters and brings some of us back to life, then he is also responsible for not saving the rest (for he made our natures, and with those natures our complete inability to swim). God, according to a logical investigation into Reformed theology, must have designed and implemented the radical outcome of Total Depravity within all our souls due to the Fall. It is God, regardless of anything we have ever said, thought or done, who put us on the bottom of the sea.

So I wondered, with the seeming unfairness of this doctrine, why are Calvinists so adamant about their ideas in this area? These are sincere Christ-followers, so there must be a goal in mind.

That goal is our avoidance of one thing – spiritual boasting.

St. Paul in his letters warns his readers against pride (rightfully) and boasting (rightfully). The Reformers worry that if we maintain that we have even the slightest thing to do with our salvation – such as our acceptance of his grace – then we have something to boast about. Many Evangelical pastors I have heard attack Catholics for, among others, the sacraments and good works we do as being non-Christian in that the accomplishment of these activities would naturally 'puff us up.'

Biblically, however, we Christ followers do have something to boast about.

Let us first go back to the context of Paul's clearest writing on this subject of resisting our proud and boastful natures.

> For it is by grace you have been saved, through faith
> – and this is not from yourself, it is a gift of God – not
> by works, so that *no one can boast*. Eph. 2:8-9.

But Paul's next words provide the context to define his term, 'works.' It is clear that in his mind, as we've seen elsewhere in the New Testament, 'works' here referred to the rules of the Old Testament Law, a law now superseded by the new Christian faith that would bring Gentile and Jew together. The Jews would no longer boast in their adherence to the works of a law that was incapable, by itself, of bringing salvation.

> Therefore, remember that formerly you who are Gentiles by birth and called 'uncircumcised' by those who call themselves 'the circumcision' (which is done in the body by human hands) – remember that at that time you were separate from Christ, excluded from citizenship in Israel and foreigners to the covenants of the promise, without hope and without God in the world...by setting aside in his flesh the Law with its commands and regulations. His purpose was to create in himself one new humanity out of the two, thus making peace, and in one body to reconcile both of them to God through the cross, by which he put to death their hostility. (Eph. 2:11-18)

Jesus himself tells us in the parable about the three servants how the master commends the first worker as his 'good and faithful servant.' This was not due to this servant's 'faith,' it was due to his actions with the resources given to him. Jesus also commends certain early local churches for their actions, as we reviewed in our discussion about Revelation.

Paul, himself, does not rule out correct pride and boasting, which has to do with our conduct (actions) in the world.

Now this is our boast: Our conscience testifies that we have conducted ourselves in the world, and especially in our relations with you, with integrity and godly sincerity. (2 Cor 1:12)

Boast then in the Lord and in the actions he helps us undertake in his service. Fight the urge to boast about ourselves falsely, but do not let this concern act as a wedge against Christians who try to build and maintain their faith through 'works' such as the Sacraments, the study of scripture, or helping those in need.

We, however, will not boast beyond proper limits, but will confine our boasting to the sphere of service God himself has assigned to us, a sphere that also includes you. (2 Cor. 10:13)

11:8   The Parable of the Sower

One of the most telling parables with regard to our discussions is also one of the most well-known. Many people call it the parable of the Soils, but others call it the parable of the Sower. Theologically, even the different names point out important issues. Jesus certainly told this story to reflect truths about us, the soils. But he also revealed truth about himself, the Father and the Spirit (the Sower) as well.

We all know the story: the Sower spreads seed (the 'word')

across four different soils, and the soils respond to the seed and produce different crops accordingly. In the Calvinist Bible (we'll call it Version 2.0), we read,

A farmer went out to sow seed. He walked past a dirt path, and a rocky place, and a third area with thorns. From the time he bought this land, the farmer decided not to break up the tightly compacted dirt on the path, or remove the rocks from their places, or cut down the thorny bushes where they grew. He finally came to a nice garden area with soil he had prepared from all eternity with good water and plentiful sunlight, and he spread his seed there where it produced a crop—a hundred, sixty or thirty times what was sown. Whoever my Father decided to place in this land and understand my words, welcome to my family. For the rest of you, better luck next time. (Mt. 13:3-9, Calvinist Version 2.0)

Jesus' explanation of this parable – as written in the Calvinist Bible – to his Apostles is critical. Following in the path laid out for us by TULIP, Christ explains to Peter and the rest,

Don't you understand this parable? Of course you do, for you are part of the elect otherwise you could not follow me as my disciples. Just as you are part of the elect, the Father has spread the seed of the Holy Spirit into the good soil of your souls. He is Sovereign and all-powerful so when he comes across a soul that Satan has taken, or one that is tied up with the cares of the world, or a soul that, in its Total Depravity, will be easily turned aside by persecution, the Father keeps the seed of faith in his satchel, only taking is out and spreading it into the Good Soil of the souls of the elect. (Mt. 13:13-20, Calvinist Version 2.0)

However, in my NIV Bible, this is not what Jesus taught his followers, nor what I believe he is teaching us. When we read about this parable in the actual scriptures (let's call it Version 1.0), we find this explanation from the Lord to his inner circle:

Don't you understand this parable? How then will you understand any parable? The farmer sows the word. Some people are like seed along the path, where the word is sown. As soon as they hear it, Satan comes and takes away the word that was sown in them. Others, like seed sown on rocky places, hear the word and at once receive it with joy. But since they have no root, they last only a short time. When trouble or persecution comes because of the word, they quickly fall away. Still others, like seed sown among thorns, hear the word; but the worries of this life, the deceitfulness of wealth and the desires for other things come in and choke the word, making it unfruitful. Others, like seed sown on good soil, hear the word, accept it, and produce a crop—some thirty, some sixty, some a hundred times what was sown. (Mt. 13:13-20)

A couple of interesting points from Jesus' explanation help with our discussion. First, the seed is the same and is *spread throughout all* of the soils. In other words, God does not predestine any soil to not receive his word. Second, for many who eventually fall away, the seed grows within their hearts and souls for a while – some even receive God's call with *joy* – before being later rejected due to various reasons such as the cares of the world, or the pressures of persecutions.

Now, the keys to Calvinism are a pair of propositions. First, we are all born Totally Depraved. We have no desire and no way of moving even the tiniest of steps toward God. We have no good in our hearts.

Second, those who express belief have been given this faith entirely by God and they will then be forevermore protected by God and never lose their faith. In this vein, perhaps, they might be seen as those in this parable who have been given good soil and produce thirty, fifty, or a hundred-fold.

The questions I have always had concern those in between. For example, our Lord tells us there are some in whom the seed grows but the roots are weak, and others who might have roots of faith growing within them, but then they lose their faith due to their cares for the world.

But, if the people in these two groups have come to any level of faith, according to Calvinist thought, that faith had to be brought about by the Holy Spirit. These people cannot have made even the first faltering steps toward God on their own. But those represented by both soils show the immediate effects of regeneration, but then do fall away. We are suddenly faced with the reality of *three* groups, not two. There are no longer the elect and the reprobate. We are now divided among the elect, the reprobate and those who are ***teased***. The teased are those whom God at first started to elect but, then, well… he just changed his mind.

Wow. That is a very scary concept to accept. That God Almighty sends his Spirit to awaken many of us, to enable us to move along our journeys of faith, only to then drop us? This present two possibilities – either God purposefully gives what seems to be true faith to many as a first step in a plan to eventually take away that individual faith, or God grants initial faith, but he is not almighty and his plans are thwarted.

But, we might ask, does Calvinism really teach this idea of God's 'teasing' someone with false faith? Unfortunately, yes.

The founder, John Calvin, concluded this from his Sola Scriptural studies of the Bible:

Still it is correctly said, that the reprobate believe God

to be propitious to them, inasmuch as they accept the gift of reconciliation, though confusedly and without due discernment; not that they are partakers of the same faith or regeneration with the children of God; but because, under a covering of hypocrisy, they seem to have a principle of faith in common with them. Nor do I even deny that *God illumines their minds to this extent,* that they recognize his grace; but that conviction he distinguishes from the peculiar testimony which he gives to his elect in this respect, that the reprobate never attain to the full result or to fruition. When he shows himself propitious to them, it is not as if he had truly rescued them from death and taken them under his protection. He only gives them a manifestation of his present mercy.[8]

And why would God give a false faith to some, making them believe their faith is true?

But the Lord, *the better to convict them,* and leave them without excuse, instills into their minds such a sense of his goodness as can be felt without the Spirit of adoption.

Let this sink in for a moment. God, in the view of the founder of what is now called Calvinism, provides some people with a false faith, so that he can later say, 'See, you saw what real faith is like, so now when I punish you (for removing this false faith and leaving you with nothing), I am all the more justified, for I have left you no excuse.'

Calvin sensed (and deduced from his Sola Scriptura reading of the Bible) that God's punishment upon those who lack any possibility of faith due to the Total Depravity in which they were born would be difficult to explain or defend. So, he concluded that God gives many people a measure of faith. Through this faith – which the person involved believes is true faith in Christ – the person senses something about the truths and goodness of God. Then, when this faith is snatched away and the person falls from faith, God has an even 'better' justification for convicting them and damning them to hell.

The problems with this theology are self-evident, but rarely taught. It obliterates the idea of 'once-saved, always saved' and the 'assurance of salvation,' for no Christian can ever know if they are living with true faith, or false faith. The doctrine of the Perseverance of the Saints is destroyed because no one can point to a person (even at themselves) and claim – 'She is truly a saint.' Worst of all, by twisting Reformed theologies in such ways in an attempt to adhere to what is obviously presented in scripture, we are left with a 'god' who is sinister enough to provide just a bit of faith so as to feel self-justified in punishing the person for not receiving the full gift (from this same 'god') for complete faith.

Note – Reformed Christians will often make the

claim that the fallen-away 'Christian' was never a true Christian in the first place. This is essentially what Calvin stated above almost five hundred years ago. Their proof? Well, the person fell from faith and obedience before they died, so obviously they were not granted the correct and lasting faith in the first place. In other words, they died outside of the state of grace. Which means, in practice, the Reformed Christian is simply following basic Catholic theology. The only difference is that Catholicism blames our own choices for our fall from grace, while Calvinism shifts the blame for our doom back upon God's choice.

So, where do we go from here? Perhaps another look at this same parable, this time as written by Luke, might help.

Those on the rocky ground are the ones who receive the word with joy when they hear it, but they have no root. They believe for a while, but in the time of testing they fall away. The seed that fell among thorns stands for those who hear, but as they go on their way they are choked by life's worries, riches and pleasures, and they do not mature. But the seed on good soil stands for those with a **noble and good** heart, who hear the word, retain it, and by persevering produce a crop. (Lk 8:11-15)

A couple of interesting items jump out. First, a uniform seed (Word of God) is again spread about, and the difference in response is due to the soils the seed encounters. Some people, as we all know from personal experience, do not respond to, or later fall away from the truth. Jesus gives us two options for this reality – that the devil comes and steals the seed, or that the individuals chose an easier path once temptation and persecution arrive.

Those in the second group (soil) are similar to those who live around us every day, seemingly good-hearted people who have heard the Word and made the choice to accept it, but only to a point. As other cares, desires, and worries come, these people fail to grow in their faith. It is not clear from the parable if these people are eventually lost, that is, do they later lose their salvation? Both Luke and Mark's accounts tell us that these people simply become unfruitful and do not *mature* in their faiths.

We then read something very interesting regarding the final group, those who are the 'good soil.' We are told by Jesus that they have 'noble and good hearts.' Again, we shouldn't read into his parables excess speculation that may confuse our Lord's main point. However, the acknowledgment of 'noble and good hearts' does require that we are not all Totally Depraved. Perhaps some do have noble and good hearts that, once they are fully awakened by the seed, can produce thirty or a hundred-fold.

11.9 Repent

If you read the story about John the Baptist, you will come away with a clear understanding concerning his focus on the issue of repentance. In fact, the very first word John the Baptist utters in Matthew's Gospel is, "Repent". (Mt. 3:2)

John the Baptist vehemently attacked the Jewish leaders of the day, telling them even if they believed they were part of God's elect, that alone was not good enough. He said this 'brood of vipers' (Mt. 3:7) would become acceptable to God only through their repentance. And repentance, in this case, did not mean simply being sorry. Repentance meant, as it did for Matthew (himself once a despised and corrupt tax collector), a tangible change of heart leading to actions. John the Baptist explains this in verse 8, "*Produce fruit* in keeping with repentance" (Mt. 3:8).

But what of John's thoughts about being part of the 'elect,' as the children of Israel believed at the time? Did he believe there was a once-for-all personal righteousness due to anyone's inclusion in the nation of God's Chosen People?

"And do not think you can say to yourselves, 'We have Abraham as our father.' I tell you that out of these stones God can raise up children of Abraham." (Mt. 3:9)

Repentance is an action. Action implies a choice. Nowhere are we told that we are forced by God to repent, for as we see in Matthew, even those God considered elect in the Old Testament time, even those responsible for teaching the ways of God and leading the Jewish religion on Earth, often did not lead acceptable lives. They were still called on to repent.

The desire to undertake a life of repentance may indeed come from a love for, and faith in, God. God may come very close to us and lead us in many ways toward this faith. The strength to move forward and change one's life is ineffective if we attempt this without Christ's help. But repentance is only achievable through the choices we all face. Once we follow through upon that desire and intent for repentance, God blesses us with increased faith and strength to follow.

Jesus could have simply walked through Galilee and waited for the predestined elect to individually receive regeneration and come to him. Instead, he taught the truth and then demanded a response to that truth. He demanded repentance.

In the mind of our Lord and Savior, it seems to me, our responses to his call were always a choice, and his effort was to always make the call.

"Unless you **repent**, you too will all perish." (Lk. 13:5)

"From that time on Jesus began to preach, "**Repent**, for the kingdom of heaven has come near." (Mt. 4:17)

"Then Jesus began to denounce the towns in which most of his miracles had been performed, because they did not **repent**." (Mt. 11:20)

"The time has come," he said. "The kingdom of God has come near. **Repent** and believe the good news!" (Mk. 1:15)

"They went out and preached that people should **repent**." (Mk. 6:12)

"I have not come to call the righteous, but sinners to **repentance**." (Lk. 5:32)

"I tell you that in the same way there will be more rejoicing in heaven over one sinner who **repents** than over ninety-nine righteous persons who do not need to repent." (Lk. 15:7)

"And **repentance** for the forgiveness of sins will be preached in his name to all nations, beginning at Jerusalem." (Lk. 24:47)

Chapter 12

The Five Attributes

As I've made reference to many times, I benefitted from the challenge and privilege of living within two Christian faith communities for an extended period. I have studied both Catholic and Evangelical views regarding regeneration and salvation. Allow me, for a moment, to synthesize what may help both sides address the main concerns of the other.

We all love God and want to honor him; Father, Son, and Holy Spirit. For simplicity, I will use 'God' in this discussion, but also Father, Son, and Holy Spirit where appropriate to distinguish at least what I believe are their specific roles in our lives and redemption.

We all seem to believe God has, essentially, five traits that make him God in the Christian understanding. Other religions may believe some of these same traits hold true for their deity, but these five traits taken together have been revealed to us Christians through the Bible and evident reason.

1. *Sovereign* – God makes the rules.

2. *Omnipotent* – God can accomplish anything he wants.

3. *Omniscience* – God knows all things.

4. *Loving* – God created us and is active in the world because he 'loves' us. He desires fellowship with us and wants the ultimate best for us. Note that I did not include 'merciful' in this list, for mercy is a subset of 'love'.

5. *Fair* – God is 'just;' he is 'righteous.'

One stream of Christian theology we've discussed at length in this book is that which I have referred to as Calvinistic, or Reformed, or Evangelical. For this chapter, let us call this outlook 'exclusive.' The key tenet of this exclusive theology revolves around the idea that when God created the universe, he knew already which *specific, individual* human beings he would provide grace to, and through that grace, salvation. The rest of humanity would be individually pre-destined to eternal damnation. Those fortunate members of the elect see their status before God as exclusive to themselves and those who believe like them, with all others being enemies of God.

While there are certainly many shades of theological thought, the second general Christian position we will label here as 'inclusive.' The *inclusive* belief maintains God sovereignly set the moral rules we are all to live by and provided the capacity (grace) for each individual to begin to move toward salvation. Through our human-will cooperation, we make choices by which we can either work with or reject God's saving grace. All humans receive a call from God, and all humans can choose to cooperate, or they can decide to turn away. No one is deemed lost and beyond salvation, for we see the capacity within all of us to choose at any time throughout our lives a positive response to God's call. No Christ follower is demonized as already damned and beyond the walls of Christ's love and forgiveness simply due to their diverse belief toward one specific theory or another regarding the process of their salvation.

How, then, do these two theories – the *inclusive* and the *exclusive* – coincide with the Five Traits of God?

12.1 The Exclusive View

The exclusive view certainly upholds God's Sovereignty. This doctrine holds that God determined whether each, individually, will be forced into saving grace or face a life in which this grace is withheld.

The exclusive view also agrees with the idea that God is Omnipotent. God used his ultimate power on a moment-by-moment basis to make sure elected individuals believe, think, feel, and do what is necessary for their salvation until their moment of death.

This view also holds tightly to the idea of God's Omniscience. The belief that God designates certain individuals to membership within the elect from all of eternity past demands that he must know the outcome of every human interaction and circumstance throughout time; past, present, and future from our point of view.

The exclusive view of God may also consider him to be Loving, but here is where we hit a major snag. In the Reformed view, God loves only the elect. His eternal plan is such that the non-elect cannot ever gain true and eternal 'good.' God cannot want, desire, or will good (heaven) for those he predestined for destruction. If he does, his Omnipotence would prove irresistible and the reprobate would also receive grace leading to salvation. In practical terms, God shows his love and mercy only to a small group of predetermined individuals which he designates from the beginning of time to be his own.

Due to his, an irresistible argument follows that the Reformed God is neither just, nor fair. We reviewed some of the analogies used in attempts to explain how God is not unfair to anyone. Yet, God is not merely a supernatural being passing by earth one day and throwing a life preserver to a few individuals already drowning. He is the creator of the universe who provided souls for the reprobate which lead them, beyond their control, into the depths of the sea. God is not truly being 'fair' even to the elect; he is only indulgent. And even these who receive grace are punished through the predetermined and eternal loss of many of their loved ones. According to the set of Reformed doctrines we've reviewed, God is not fair to the 'reprobate' who are born in a way that precludes them from any opportunity for redemption.

12.2   The Inclusive View

The inclusive view holds that we each possess some level of human-will and responsibility to follow God's call. It therefore maintains that all those who claim to follow Christ have made the correct choice and should be counted by all others as brothers and sisters in the Lord. It is not the same as universalism, however; the inclusivity we speak of is among those who see Jesus as the Son of the Father and Lord of creation. How he deals with those outside this Christian faith, well, we will leave that up to God and pray for him to be merciful.

As we've discussed in length throughout this book, this inclusive view does not mean either that simple membership in a Christian faith community is enough, nor that a simple profession of faith assures an individual of eternal life.

This view is consistent with God's Sovereignty. Those holding this view believe that God, and God alone, created the plan for salvation and provided Jesus as our Savior. To reach his ultimate goal for humanity as a whole, he may also execute specific plans through individual human beings, providing grace even for some who may initially not want it, such as with Saul who became the Apostle Paul. He also makes and enforces the rules that guide our moral lives, as any earthly sovereign would do.

The inclusive view agrees that God is Omnipotent, for we believe God can, at any time, exercise his power to change history, whether it be for an individual or for our entire universe. We seek his miracles. However, the inclusive view allows for the sovereign and omnipotence of God to show itself in his choices not to interfere in our lives as well.

Where the inclusive view steps well ahead of its more exclusive cousin is in its promotion of God's love and mercy. He created us as human beings with souls possessing the human-will that makes our love of him meaningful. As CS Lewis wrote in <u>Mere Christianity</u>, we are not automatons (robots) who go through life without choice. For with no choice, there is no ability to love. And that love is both what God seeks from us and the one thing we need in order to experience the depths and heights of our ultimate happiness with him.

The Son sacrificed himself so all peoples can repent and receive forgiveness for their sins. We grow as we witness Jesus' humility and receive daily support through the Holy Spirit, who advocates for what is right. God, Three-in-One, wants to have a loving, eternal relationship with all his creatures. Those who make even the slightest choice to turn to him in continual repentance enter the community of souls provided with the pre-determined pathway, through the sacrifice of Jesus, to enter God's family.

In terms of justice and fairness, the inclusive view excels. The view promotes true human-will and therefore true human responsibility for our failures and merit for humbly returning over and again to God. With possible exceptions needed to carry out God's master plan for humanity as a whole, no one is predestined for damnation for sins they have had no choice but to commit or for lacking the faith they had been predestined not to have.

So far, we are four for four.

But what about the fifth trait of God? Is the inclusive view consistent with the idea of God's Omniscience? If, the concern is, we do have human-will, can we then do something, say something, think or even feel something that is a surprise to God? Can we validate the idea of true, meaningful human-will with the idea God has any type of predestined plan for us, individually or communally?

It is a valid and interesting question, for if we look at this issue only on a surface level, we quickly discover a problem. If God in his Omniscience foresees me, for example, eventually saved, but I actually have the human-will to choose a different path at some point in my life, can God any longer be considered Omniscient?

First, we should precisely define our term, 'Omniscient.' There are not one, but three classes of knowledge to which Omniscience can refer. God can know everything that has happened in our past. This is not difficult to understand or believe. We ourselves can know everything in history, if only we were smart enough, had enough time and/or had a nature which provides the ability to be everywhere at once. Today, especially, we can envision a security camera system that covers every inch of the world, a hard drive large enough to store all the recorded videos, and a computer smart and fast enough to interpret what's happening on all the video feeds at all times.

The same thing can be said about the second class of data and omniscient knowledge, that being the present. Knowing the present has pretty much the same considerations as knowledge of the past, it is just moving at and past us quite a bit faster.

It is the third group of data – concerning the future – however, that is the most difficult to reconcile. Since we humans are stuck in time and can barely keep up with the local environments we are stuck in during this present, it is very difficult to envision 'knowing' the future with the same level of precision with which we can know the past or even the present.

There are two things we can know, however, about the future. If we are omnipotent and sovereign, then we can know that some of the 'actual' future events will and must happen. If, for example, a king planned for his daughter to wed a prince on her 18th birthday in front of a hall full of guests, he has the power to make sure her wedding happens on that day, and his daughter is married in front of hundreds of nobles. Similarly, if God predicted at the time of Christ that, for example, the Jewish Temple would be destroyed, there are very few things he would have to change in the future to make that happen. In truth, he would only have to convince a single Roman general to undertake an attack. The proven predictions in this case does not require God to choose to universally control every moment of our lives.

The other foreknowledge one can have concerns the identity of all 'potential' future events. The same king may not have the power and sovereignty beyond his kingdom's borders to make sure that all eligible 18-year-old princes come to meet his daughter. He cannot guarantee any one of them who enters his castle will fall in love with his daughter, and vice versa. But we can understand that the more powerful the king is, the more princes he can cajole to meet the princess. The wiser he is, and with more options, the better he can predict the best match for his little girl. With additional power and wisdom, the probability that one single potentiality (that, let's say, that Prince Carlo falls in mutual love with Princes Anabelle) turns into an actuality (and future certainty) grows.

Where does this idea get us when considering an *all*-powerful and *all*-wise God? Might there be infinite potentialities from our limited perspective, possibilities that come about due to our human-will choices, but only a few, or even just one, option that to God's eyes appear as certainties?

The ideas we consider in theology come from scripture and the Traditions of the Christian Churches, but they also can be enlightened by new information. New challenges and discoveries often force the Church to rely on the Holy Spirit to bring to light new distinctions that make our knowledge more complete. Currently, we live in a scientific age, so just perhaps this scientific point of view and our new techno-logical tools might help our discussion here.

One of the seminal works in twentieth century science fiction is the <u>Foundation Series</u>, offered up by author Isaac Asimov. The story revolves around a galactic empire of trillions of people spread throughout the universe which had been at peace for a thousand years.

One scientist establishes the 'Foundation.' He recruits all types of other scientists and they come to the Foundation just as the animals came to Noah's ark. They toil at an outpost at the very edge of the galaxy, creating a great encyclopedia. In this exhaustive work will be stored all human knowledge up to that point.

Why is this work being done? Because the scientist has determined, through exhaustive statistical studies of humanity, that the empire is about to implode. Humanity will descend into a thousand-year dark age which can only be shortened and lessened by saving this treasure trove of human knowledge. Future generations will use this knowledge base to more quickly rebuild a new and stable society.

The scientists cannot predict with one hundred percent certainty the actions of any single human being but, with a trillion human samples merged together into a massive single organism, they can predict with almost perfect accuracy what will happen to the human species as a whole. In the story, the predetermined plan works like clockwork for decades. Several times as the failing empire is thrown deeper into chaos around them, the members of the Foundation are provided videos from the group's founder, along with certain 'assistance.' Each time, some piece of knowledge, technology, or advice has been left for them along with recorded instructions telling the Foundation community what should be happening to them at that particular moment in time. This aide assists the Foundation in defeating one group of upstart enemies after another. The assistance comes at almost exactly the correct times, even though the lead scientists were long since dead, because they were able to map out with statistics what would happen decades and centuries ahead of their own time.

Considering this novel, I looked at the mathematics the Foundation scientists used the theories of probability and statistical analysis which helped the predictions come true. I didn't realize that it wasn't until well into the sixteen-hundreds that the concept of probability came into existence. So, when our forefathers at the time of the Reformation contrasted various ideas of salvation and how to define God's Omniscience, the concepts of probability we now take for granted were in their infancy.

You can see the analogy. If God knows all the potential outcomes, and knows through his wisdom the *probability* that each potential outcome will become an actuality, then he can 'know' the future without having to use his Omnipotence to *make* that future happen outside of our human-wills. He may have entered history in special ways for individuals like Mary and Peter without requiring that every detail of every human life be forced upon the rest of us. He could, for example, have known that a young Hebrew woman possessed a personality that would almost certainly lead her to accept the request of the angel to bring the Savior into the world without having to predestine or force her to follow that path. He could have known that Peter's personality and desires would have made him the perfect leader of the infant church, a knowledge made all the more perfect and sure each time Jesus taught him another lesson during their time together.

If this is true, then we can reconcile the ideas of God's Omniscience with his fairness and mercy. He, through his own free-will, provides common graces to everyone who, through their own human-wills, either respond to his calls or reject him. He can also will to provide extraordinary grace (the very definition of a 'miracle') for some individuals to bring about his overall Sovereign plan without being backed into the corner in which he needs to irresistibly save some and irresistibly damn others and control every moment of the lives of every soul ever born.

Does God, in this case, have complete and Omniscient knowledge concerning the eternal fate of every human being? I believe so, but perhaps others would argue the case. For myself at least, demanding absolute foreknowledge so severely damages the traits of Love, Mercy, Righteousness, and

Fairness that it is a minor sacrifice to take a shade or two off God's knowledge of the future. In other words, the inclusive view honors four of God's traits completely, and most of the fifth. This view also maintains one of our core human, God-given traits, the existence of our wills.

For if God knew from all eternity that only specific individuals would be part of his elect, it would require complete control over macro-issues such as the survival of all of those individuals' ancestors, the meeting and emotional responses of their parents, the locations of their births and upbringings, etc. It would also require complete control over the micro-issues within the individual, such as that person's deepest sense of personality, which will lead to a certain emotional response to the grace needed for salvation.

I can imagine God searching me as a fully formed adult and predicting through his perfect sense of probability (out of all of my 'potentialities') where I am bound to go, even while ensuring at least some level of human-will. But to know this spiritual destiny from all eternity – again, admitting to the special 'miraculous' interventions he may provide that nudge some of us forcefully in the right direction – God must literally know our personality before we are in the womb. This personality must of itself also be precisely developed in the unborn child by God. And so, some unborn children are, even in that pre-birth state, already moving toward heaven irresistibly while other unborn babies are already moving toward hell.

12.3 The Practical Outcome

What is the practical view, then, of our understanding of God's Five Traits?

If God has predestined each of us individually and eternally for either salvation or damnation, and if he chooses to grant salvific grace only to a small 'elect' who believe in a specific set of doctrines irresistibly, then the Calvinist claim of 'once saved, always saved' is actually far too mild. The truth would simply be, '*always saved*'.

If elect, we would not experience a point of time in our lives when we aren't saved, so there is no 'once' involved. There would never be a time before which we weren't saved and then, afterward, we were saved. From God's eternal point of view, we were always saved, and any profession of faith or other activity on our part is destined to happen and really only a matter of formality. The elect do not, in a strict sense, need to go to church. They do not need to read the Bible. They do not need to carry on any spiritual discipline or activity. They are already chosen by God for salvation.

They cannot even die prior to coming to faith in Christ. They – *cannot*. It is an impossibility.

And while they cannot die before God grants them the required predestined faith (and understanding of true Christian doctrine), no one who doesn't believe exactly as they do – no one who is predestined for damnation - can ever die in a state of salvific faith. The most seemingly loving, pious, God-fearing, Christ-adoring, Spirit-trusting Trinitarian believing individual in the world cannot – *cannot* – live a moment – not ONE MOMENT – with any of that truth. Any glimmer of faith they have in mind or express in action has only been given to them (being Totally Depraved) by God as a farce (for only God can regenerate in the slightest way), and true faith would be both irresistible and eternal (for TULIP to be correct).

Thus, professing Christ-followers are divided as natural enemies – those born already saved and devoted to God, and those so hated by God that, despite thinking they love Christ, are still doomed, always have been, and always will be. If God so hated most of the world, then those who consider themselves the few elect (the few loved ones) can only be faithful followers by doing the same.

The Inclusive view, on the other hand, maintains that we are all called (and loved) by God, our common Creator. Perhaps some find God's invitation nearly irresistible to ignore, and yet we all have the level of freedom necessary to truly accept or truly reject that call. Even after our initial conversion and baptism into the faith, we still can equally sin. Each sin is a small (or large) but true rejection of Christ. We must then repent again as our Savior commanded and return humbly again into the family of God. On the other hand, we (each and all of us) can live inside our prideful rebellion and grow more and more distant from Jesus.

The Inclusive view, then, demands we engage in those

spiritual disciplines which can bring us ever closer to God and changes the potentiality for our salvation into an actuality. As CS Lewis wrote, again in <u>Mere Christianity</u>, "every time you make a choice you are turning the central part of you, the part of you that chooses, into something a little different from what it was before. And taking your life as a whole, with all your innumerable choices, all your life long you are slowly turning this central thing either into a heavenly creature or into a hellish creature…Each of us at each moment is progressing to the one state or the other."

We are all, biblically, on this path progressing toward one state or the other, and none of us should claim 'God loves me and hates you.'

Chapter 13

A Flowering Faith

Let us assume for the moment that the arguments laid out in this book are correct and there are two plausible interpretations of the verses used to support the idea of Predestined Individual Election. Let us say furthermore that the second (inclusive) interpretation enables us to validate and defend several very important characteristics of our God, including kindness, love, forgiveness, mercy, fairness, and justice. The second interpretation also enables all of us as Christians to see fellow Christ-followers as potential allies, potential eternal co-habitants in heaven, even if they err in some doctrine or practice.

Even so, it would be difficult for believers in a more exclusive Reformed Christian theology to make the mental transition to the second alternative. Many people have been brought up with the understanding of an eternally pre-destined election for each individual. They have been taught the Five Points of Calvinism, whether or not they use those specific terms, and no matter how strongly these concepts are turned aside by scripture, a change in view is very difficult.

As a Catholic who learned about the concepts behind TULIP later in life, perhaps I can offer another alternative. The hang-up seems to come primarily from our definitions of predestination. Some believe from their reading of scripture that there are some predestined for faith and other predestined for failure. It is difficult to consider the term predestined without thinking about who did the predestining. In other words, using the term 'predestined' implies an action, and since we cannot predestine ourselves to anything, God must have been the one who predestined.

However, if we look at the engineers, for example, at Ford Motor Company who build a car to certain set of specifications using certain tools and materials, every one of them knows that every car they construct will someday fail. We can say that these engineers *predestined* failed cars the moment they decided to build the cars. No car can be designed and built to work forever, perfectly.

Similarly, we can rightly say that God predestined us for failure as individuals and as a species. But that failure only came in terms of his giving us certain specifications, in this case human-will, in the first place.

Knowing we would fail due to our natural 'specifications,' God used his sovereign will and all-powerful nature to develop a plan for our salvation. He did this out of his love for each of us. Christ would come to earth to sacrifice himself for the forgiveness of our sins and to provide an example for living in proper humility before the Trinity. Those who use their human-will specifications to follow Christ are working with God to modify their natural specifications, to become more like Christ themselves. Those who join and remain within the community of these Christ-like persons are then predestined, due to their changed and improved(ing) specifications, to make it to heaven.

For those who agree with the arguments discussed in this book, that there is enough evidence from scripture to support the inclusive view of salvation that brings together Christian believers, let us take a moment to think about what that doctrine would mean in terms of the Five Points of Calvinism. If we can discuss TULIP in Reformed terms so that all Christians might discover common ground, we can grow together in one family of Christ, as did the early Jewish and Gentile converts to the faith.

The first of the five points, as we discussed, is the idea of Total Depravity. This is a difficult concept if one believes in Communal Predestined Election. If we are to believe in human-will in the slightest, we must believe we are spiritually injured, but not dead, because a dead person has no human-will. To be consistent with scripture, perhaps we can change the 'T' to 'transitory' or 'temporary' depravity. This will remind us that by ourselves, without the help of God, we cannot live perfect enough lives to demand eternity with God in heaven. But, in the face of the saving grace provided by Jesus Christ, our depravity must be looked at as a *transitory* thing. A *temporary* condition that lasts only as long as we refuse to repent and take the first small steps toward our God.

In terms of Unconditional Election, there really is no problem in maintaining that term. God *set the plan* for our salvation, and he carries it out. This plan did not come about because we as humans met any preconditions. The plan came about through God's love for us. We must see this unconditional election as being God's determination to elect those who move toward his faith community. Our individual salvation is not unconditional (even the strictest Calvinist believes in the 'condition' of faith), but God's loving plan and offer of salvation is.

What about 'Limited Atonement'? Here we must make some alterations to the Reformed view.

In order to support and defend the all-powerful nature of our Savior, we must never restrict the efficiency and effectiveness of his sacrifice. His sacrifice is enough to save the entire world. If every human being in the world chose to follow him, there is no limit to the amount of grace that will come through his sacrifice. Since we know there will always be two groups of people, those who freely choose to follow Jesus and those who freely choose to not follow him, we can still maintain the 'L' in Limited Atonement because saving grace only is effecttive for those who make the right decisions and join the community of Christians.

However, to properly reflect Jesus as the Son 'through whom all things were made,' there can be nothing to limit Christ's love for his human race.

Which brings us to Irresistible Grace. To properly reflect scripture and our real-life experiences, perhaps all we must do is simply redefine who we point to as receiving grace irresistibly. There are certainly those who proclaim faith in Christ, who – from our point of view – must be considered people covered by God's grace, who then fall away, never to return. The application of irresistible grace, therefore, cannot be universal upon all peoples, or even all professed Christians.

That said, God has clearly called various people throughout time and provided them with specific graces for specific purposes at specific times. These purposes may have universal effects such as Mary's being called to birth the Savior, or they may have only personal outcomes such God's powerful conversion of Saul into the Apostle Paul. Perhaps Mary could not have rejected the Motherhood of Jesus. Perhaps Paul had to be the one-time persecutor turned theologian and missionary. Perhaps an all-powerful God can express his power in some specific points in specific lives without doing away with the near-universal gift of human-will and moral responsibility. Perhaps we can change this concept to 'specific' irresistible grace in order to smooth the path from an exclusive view of the faith to a more inclusive view toward all who claim Jesus as Lord and Savior.

Finally, what about the Perseverance of the Saints? In many ways, this was really the goal of Luther. He wanted to know for sure he would be saved, especially having rejected the Church he had grown up in. He found his concerns relieved by the idea that once he came to a specific type of faith in Christ, God would preserve him for all eternity. As we discussed, however, this 'preservation' or 'perseverance' goes against evident reason, real-life experiences, and the scriptures (as we saw with Calvin's comments about those I called the 'teased'). The idea of 'preservation' can be maintained, however, if we consider God's protection of the saints from a communal perspective.

In other words, God set in motion the plan through which he will save everyone – without exception – who continue to respond to his grace through their human-wills and enter the Christian community. While living with Christ, however, we may occasionally lose or damage our faith through sin. If we thereafter repent and reenter the community of faith, the Body of Christ, God will accept us. He will not today say that those who believe in Christ will be forgiven of their sins and tomorrow change his mind and only forgive those people who speak Russian.

God – Father, Son, and Holy Spirit – will preserve those saints who persevere to the end. They will then, as Paul wrote, not be 'disqualified for the prize' (1 Cor. 9:27).

As we've discussed earlier, people on both sides of these debates are passionate to defend certain attributes of God. For those traditionally defined as being on the Calvinistic end of the spectrum, the ideas I summarized in Predestined Individual Election are used to promote God's sovereignty, his almighty power, and his omniscient wisdom. As a Catholic entering the Evangelical environment, however, I found this theology to be at odds with other attributes of our Father, namely fairness, love, forgiveness, and justice. I believe Paul and the rest of the New Testament writers shared a critical goal to tell their readers that, regardless of their background, they all had been given the choice to enter the community of believers. Those who chose this new Christian 'body' and remained in God's grace through faith and obedience – these then benefitted from the predestined plan of redemption through Jesus Christ.

Once we accept this view of scripture, we can better accept each other. We can look clear-headedly at the main purpose for the Christian Community. That is, how can we and our brethren – whether through sacraments, biblical study, evangelization, missions, small groups, etc. – best make the correct choices through faith to Christ? Can we, through spiritual disciplines, better remain in a state of repentance and saving grace throughout our own personal lives and remain predestined for eternal bliss?

We, then, as Catholic parents, children, friends, and family, better understand the background of the Reformation and how Reformed doctrines grew out of the psychological requirements of those who sought to leave the Church. We discovered that the 'Five Solas,' the Reformation slogans still used today to drive a wedge between Catholics and our faith, do not represent either biblical or historical Christianity. Finally, we have found not only that the specific Biblical verses used by others to challenge our faith do not actually represent the 'Doctrines of Grace' or the tenets of Predestined Individual Election. Instead, the scriptures as a whole, and especially the precious words of our Lord himself, point to the more inclusive view of the Christian faith we celebrate within Catholicism to this very day.

THE END

SELECTED REFERENCES

(1) https://www.sjsu.edu/people/james.lindahl/courses/Hum1B/s3/Luther-Speech-Worms-1521.pdf Note, other translations use 'evident reason', and some use 'and' instead of 'or'.

(2) MacArthur, John F. The Gospel According to Jesus. Zondervan. Kindle Edition. Location 304.

(3) https://catholic-resources.org/Lectionary/Statistics.htm

(4) http://www.usccb.org/beliefs-and-teachings/what-we-believe/

(5) http://www.trinitylutheranms.org/MartinLuther/TowerExperience.html

(6) https://zondervanacademic.com/blog/martin-luther-james-Bible

(7) Augustine, Saint. The Complete Works of Saint Augustine (Kindle Location 131333).

(8) Institutes of the Christian Religion, John Calvin, Book 3, Chapter 2, Section 11

Concerning the Definition of Evangelicalism

A) It is difficult even for self-proclaimed Evangelicals

to clearly define who belongs within their fellowship. This lack of clarity, however, cannot prevent us from engaging with the arguments made by the leaders of this movement. One interesting set of information regarding the history and present form of Evangelicalism is found on the website for Wheaton College (http://www.wheaton.edu/isae/defining-evangelicalism).

B) One of the largest 'Bible' churches in America does not explicitly list 'Calvinism' or TULIP on their website, and yet, buried within the Doctrinal Statement is the following '*All human beings, therefore, are totally depraved by nature and by choice*' and '*Before Creation, God chose those who would be saved and granted this unearned grace solely based on His sovereign good pleasure*'. These are two of the five *Doctrines of Grace* from the Calvinist tradition as summarized by TULIP.
https://harvestbiblechapel.org/what-we-believe/doctrinal-statement/

FIVE POINTS OF CALVINISM
(From http://www.calvinistcorner.com/tulip.htm)

Calvinism is known by an acronym: T.U.L.I.P.

1. **T**otal Depravity
2. **U**nconditional Election
3. **L**imited Atonement (also known as Particular Atonement)
4. **I**rresistible Grace
5. **P**erseverance of the Saints (also known as Once Saved Always Saved)

Note - there are those who consider themselves, for example, *'Four Point' Calvinists* who de-emphasize or disbelieve altogether one of these Five Points, but in the main, these five ideas best define the Reformed beliefs that separate the elect and the lost.

PIE –   Predestined Individual Election –

The concept that God predestined from the beginning of time the election (through regeneration) only certain individuals to be saved to eternal life.

CPE -   Communal Predestined Election –

The concept that God predestined a plan to offer all individuals who join and remain within the community of believers.

FIVE SOLAS OF THE REFORMATION

(From http://www.christianity.com/church/church-history/the-five-solas-of-the-protestant-reformation.html)

1. ***Sola Scriptura*** ("scripture alone"): The Bible alone is our highest authority.
2. ***Sola Fide*** ("faith alone"): We are saved through faith alone in Jesus Christ.
3. ***Sola Gratia*** ("grace alone"): We are saved by the grace of God alone.
4. ***Solus Christus*** ("Christ alone"): Jesus Christ alone is our Lord, Savior, and King.
5. ***Soli Deo Gloria*** ("to the glory of God alone"): We live for the glory of God alone.

Selected Old Testament Uses of 'Jacob' in Place of 'Israel'

(One reference shown per book for brevity)

Num. 23:7	Ez. 39.25
Deut. 32:9, 33:4	Hos. 12:2
1 Sam. 12:8	Am. 6:8
1 Chron. 16:17	Ob. 1:17
Psa. 14:7	Mic. 1:5
Is. 41:8	Jer. 26:10

Appendix A: A Brief Look at Mary and Purgatory

When my three children were born, they were baptized into the Christian faith at our Catholic Parish. My two older children went on to receive first Communion. Around this time, we also attended an Evangelical church on a part-time basis.

My understanding of Evangelical/Reformed Christianity grew along with my appreciation for the enthusiasm and seriousness of these Christians. Like most Americans, I had been brought up to appreciate reading and studying, so the in-depth sermons (or seminars) during Evangelical services held a certain appeal. Naturally, due to the 'newness' of the experience, I also found a freshness and excitement coursing through these Christian events. I was not there simply in a passive role doing my duty to my family, I was engaged and learning.

At first, we split time every other week between our two churches. I also listened, almost on a daily basis, to various Evangelical preachers on the radio and waded through the associated websites that matched up with their ministries.

The longer I went and the more I listened, the more deeply I thought about the issues these Christians found problematic with my Catholic faith. I also recognized there are concepts within Evangelical teaching that were deeply inconsistent. These doctrines were not purposefully misleading in most cases, but they were items that - perhaps due to my 'Catholic ears' - I heard differently from those who had lived in those Christian circles since birth. I also spent many long hours poring over the details of the *Catechism of the Catholic Church* (*CCC*) in an effort to better understand my own faith and to investigate whether the challenges I now heard were true or just the result of misunderstandings or ignorance.

While I understand there are certainly, now and in the past, Catholics who have been violently against Evangelical or Protestant Christianity, in my fifty-plus years of personal experience at multiple Catholic Parishes, church school environments, and Masses, I rarely if ever heard a negative comment toward our Protestant brothers. In fact, it is very clearly stated in the *Catechism*, the official teaching of the Catholic faith, that we acknowledge these Christian brothers are baptized into the Trinitarian, universal church, although not in 'full communion' or living out the 'full expression' of Christ's plan for us.

The same level of acceptance certainly did not hold true when my family went to Evangelical services. At the churches we attended, the pastors often called people forward on a regular basis to tell of their faith stories. Many, implicitly or explicitly, made the point that Catholics are not saved. One told of a father, a life-long Catholic, who finally on his death bed 'accepted Christ and was saved.' Another told of a mission trip taken to a locale where the missionaries saw many people 'coming to the faith.' Where had these missionaries gone? Not to Taoist Asia, not to the Muslim Middle East, nor to an old communist state like Russia. No, this mission trip was to Mexico, the aim evidently to 'save' a population already 80-90% Christian, or at least 80-90% Catholic.

I understood these seeming contradictions (for example, trying to 'convert' Christ-followers to Christianity) came out of a background of misunderstanding, but I felt a growing trepidation in terms of what my attendance at these Evangelical churches would mean to me and my children's walk with Christ. For the first time, I worried about profound questions like, "Dad, why are they saying that our church is wrong? Does the Bible actually say we aren't saved? What about grandma and grandpa and all the others we care about who are Catholics?"

The importance of these questions forced me to deeply reconsider what I believed and led me to put on to paper for my children those items I found to support the fundamental Scriptural and historical foundations for the Catholic faith. In a world where our children face the tyranny of indifference, I wanted to teach them to care, to take an active role in their world even when they see people of faith arguing and insisting one another are lost. What do we tell them when religious leaders maintain that those not exactly in lock-step with them are part of the 'non-elect,' a group destined – or rather *eternally pre-destined* by God – for damnation? Eternal enemies of one another.

My focus was to lay out the case for 'fundamentalist'

Christians to understand it is truly the Catholic faith, initiated by Christ through the Apostles and maintained by the Holy Spirit for two thousand years which is, by definition, the fundamental Christian church. That, in fact, this universal (catholic) Church was led by the Holy Spirit in the fourth and fifth centuries to define the basic truths of our shared Christian faith against the dangerous heresies of the time. These truths, now commonly accepted by most Evangelical brothers in the faith, were codified in the Nicene Creed[4] and repeated by every Catholic in Mass seventeen hundred years later.

Further, that the same clergy and church hierarchy during these centuries were chosen by the Holy Spirit to codify the New Testament Scriptures, choosing from among the writings used within the various churches only those now regarded by all of us as the inspired New Testament. It is hard to imagine basing a theology on 'sola scriptura' and then using that theology to insist that the Catholic Church is not Christian at all.

Lastly, that the same Catholic leadership called by God to establish the Creed and establish the Canon of accepted Scriptures also shared one final thing with today's Catholics, a third leg holding up all of the Christian life - the sacramental system. Why, I thought, would the Holy Spirit give to these fourth-century Catholics bishops and theologians arguably the most critical tasks ever given to a human being (beyond the work of the original Twelve Apostles) and still allow these leaders to lead the Church into a false form of worship?

Through the fog of time and the distrust bred from the conflicts of the Reformation, this same Catholic Church is greatly misunderstood by Evangelicals. As misunderstanding is often the first step leading toward distrust, let us discuss two example considerations of Catholic beliefs before getting into the Book of Romans.

I spent a few paragraphs in the previous chapters laying out for my fellow Catholics the basics of Calvinist thought so as to clear away some of our own misunderstandings. So, too, let us next discuss two points of the Catholic faith that are often condemned by those outside the Church. Perhaps, once these examples are correctly understood (though not necessarily agreed-with), we can consider together from a position of mutual trust the Scriptural proofs, one way or the other, concerning the more critical and divisive issue of Predestined Individual Election.

A.1 Mary

Some may read the title of this section and assume, 'of course, the author is raised Catholic, so he will focus upon Mary.' No. The reason for beginning with Mary is not due to any preeminent position she holds in the life of Catholics like me, but because a large part of the Evangelical challenge raised against Catholicism is based upon false or misrepresented statements regarding the Mother of God.

I have great respect for the now late Pastor RC Sproul, who was alive during the writing of this book. In a radio sermon called 'The Virgin Mary,' he stated that the Hail Mary (which many Protestants hold as being nearly heretical) is 'at the heart of the liturgy of the Roman Catholic Church.' Now, the liturgy is more commonly equated to the Mass, and as such, Pastor Sproul's statement is entirely false. The Hail Mary, and indeed Mary herself, are in no way the central theme of the Mass. But the statement Pastor Sproul made feeds into the general accusation that the Church of Rome holds Mary in a position above Jesus. On the surface, some of the various titles given to her over the centuries, the 'Queen of Heaven,' for example, gives the impression that Mary sits on the throne next to God the Father (the 'King of Heaven'), with Jesus playing, I suppose, the part of Crown Prince.

Another misconception that has gained traction is the idea that Catholics 'pray' to Mary and not to Christ; that we ask Mary for forgiveness, and not Christ; that we are told to worship her, instead of our Lord. This is a result of the common Evangelical definition of 'prayer' being different from the Catholic understanding. In our Evangelical church we were taught 'ACTS' form proper prayer, that we are to *Adore* God, *Confess* our sins, give *Thanks*, and then ask for what we need in *Supplication*. These steps have no place in the Catholic view of 'praying' to Mary. 'Prayer' in this case is not worship; it is communication. And we 'communicate' our requests to her to intercede through her Son on our behalf. Now, we may debate whether those in heaven can hear those requests and act upon them, but we deny the biblical and historical proofs that we are all called to intercede in prayer for one another.

My initial response when I heard these attacks was to consider the most important part of my faith life, that being the Catholic Mass. It will almost undoubtedly surprise most non-Catholics to discover there are only a few brief mentions of Mary during the entire celebration. We ask her, *along with* the other saints and our living brothers and sisters, to pray to God (Father, Son, and Holy Spirit) on our behalf. We also recite the Nicene Creed which has only six short words in reference to Mary ('was incarnate of the Virgin Mary'), all having to do with Jesus, her son. It is this same Nicene Creed, developed by the Church almost seventeen hundred years ago, that put to bed vital questions such as the divinity of Christ and is followed by nearly a majority of Christians to this day.

But, perhaps, what we find in the official statement called *Lumen Gentium* that came out of the Vatican II Council means more than anything I can put to paper. (Before I begin to quote sources such as this and Holy Scripture, please note that all italics or bold items are added by me for emphasis.)

> There is one God, and there is one mediator between God and human beings, the man Christ Jesus who gave himself as a ransom for them all" (1 Tim 2:5-6). Now, the maternal role of Mary towards humanity in no way obscures or diminishes the unique mediation of Christ; rather it shown for its power. ...it flows forth from the superabundance of Christ's merits, is founded on his mediation, completely depends on this and from this draws all its power; it in no way hinders the direct union of believers with Christ; rather it fosters this union. (Paragraph 60)

There is no additional context to be read into this statement that can diminish its straightforward point. But, for those still worried, the Catholic Church presses this point in the *Catechism*,

> Mary's function as mother of men in no way obscures or diminishes this unique mediation of Christ, but rather shows its power." (*CCC*, Paragraph 970)

I personally suffered with several questions over the years regarding the Church's beliefs regarding Mary. Are we to believe she is somehow omnipresent? In other words, if many of us communicate with her at once, can she hear all our pleas for intercession? Is she omniscient? In other words, if we ask her to pray to Jesus for a specific request, does she know all of the circumstances surrounding that request? In the same vein, how does she determine which requests to intercede for?

I believe these types of questions are the primary reason for Tradition. All Christian denominations have their own Traditions, their own particular way of interpreting Scripture and the issues of faith. For me, I know all too well there are levels to questions that go beyond my own thoughts and preferences, levels of answers that go far beyond my own wisdom. But the Holy Spirit, using the best and brightest of the best and brightest for the past two thousand years has answered these questions. Even if those answers are unknown or unknowable to me, I must begin from the point of view that I am to believe.

But clearly, the core Catholic belief in the role of Mary is far from the stereotype held and taught by far too many Evangelicals. She is not a goddess; she does not grant us forgiveness or anything out of her own power. She is concerned for us as members of her Son's Body, and she will intercede with God on our behalf through that same Son to help bring about his kingdom.

A.2 Purgatory

Many Evangelicals also criticize the Catholic Church by insisting it teaches that we can buy our way into heaven from purgatory. The Catholic Church, we are told, steal from the faithful by assuring us that we can pay to receive *indulgences* (forgiveness) from our sins. These indulgences supposedly obligate God to forgive us, or our loved ones, so we essentially buy passage out of hell and into heaven.

This was a very critical issue in the 1500s. In a very real way, the entire Reformation was sparked from criticisms concerning indulgences. However, the issues initially raised by Martin Luther were soon lost after multiple voices grew in protest to the Church. While a study of Martin Luther's famous 95 Theses prove not only did Luther believe in the concept of Purgatory, and even in the theory of Indulgences, his deep criticism over the *practice* of indulgences in his time and place eventually led to a split within the Body of Christ.

For my Evangelical brethren, let me assure them first of this – the Catholic faith does not teach that Purgatory is a place where sinful people who do not believe in Christ go to receive a 'second chance.' It is instead a place where *believers*, who are already destined to go to heaven, are purified of their sinful natures.

The early Christian faith faced an obvious question – since human beings are not instantly perfected when they claim faith in Jesus (just look within ourselves), and no one claims the process of dying perfects us immediately upon taking our last breath, we have a dilemma. Most Christians agree that the repentant person who believes in Jesus as Lord and trusts him for forgiveness as Savior will enter heaven at some point. But, the Bible clearly states that nothing impure can spend eternity with a Holy God in heaven (or, to be slightly more self-centered, who among us wants to spend such an eternity with the muck and stain, anger and lusts, that we all currently suffer from?).

To solve this challenge, the Church over time concluded there must be a place, or a state, in which we are purified after death. Several Scriptural references seem to support this idea, but the main reason this doctrine has been accepted is that it simply follows Luther's 16th Century rule that it is 'evidently reasonable.'

Now, we can all certainly agree that at some point between Christ and Luther one of more practices of the Church regarding indulgences (and therefore the truest understanding about purgatory) went off-track. In fact, the Catholic Council of Trent in the mid-1500's corrected the very practices Luther protested against protested in terms of the sale of indulgences.

In granting them (*indulgences*), however, it desires
that, in accordance with the ancient and approved
custom in the Church, moderation be observed; lest,
by excessive facility, ecclesiastical discipline be

enervated. And being desirous that the abuses which have crept therein, and by occasion of which this honorable name of Indulgences is blasphemed by heretics, be amended and corrected, it ordains generally by this decree, that *all evil gains* for the obtaining thereof, - whence a most prolific cause of abuses amongst the Christian people has been derived, - *be wholly abolished*....that, after having been reviewed by the opinions of the other bishops also, they may forthwith be referred to the Sovereign Roman Pontiff, by whose authority and prudence that which may be expedient for the universal Church will be ordained; that this the gift of holy Indulgences may be dispensed to all the faithful, piously, holily, and incorruptly. (Council of Trent, 25th Session, 21st Chapter)

In terms of the theology behind the idea of purgatory, let us look at St Augustine, the Catholic church father whose writings are interpreted by Evangelicals as providing support and proof for their ideas like Predestined Personal Election, let us read at least a bit from the North African as to his fourth century thoughts on purgatory:

Augustine:

But by the prayers of the holy Church, and by the

salvific sacrifice, and by the alms which are given for their spirits, there is no doubt that the dead are aided, that the Lord might deal more mercifully with them than their sins would deserve.... It is not at all to be doubted that such prayers are of profit to the dead; but for such of them as lived before their death in a way that makes it possible for these things to be useful to them after death, (Sermon 172:2).

Temporal punishments are suffered by some in this life only, by some after death, by some both here and hereafter, but all of them before that last and strictest judgment. But not all who suffer temporal punishments after death will come to eternal punishments, which are to follow after that judgment, (The City of God Book 21 Chapter 13 [A.D. 419]).

Nor can it be denied that the souls of the dead find relief through the piety of their friends and relatives who are still alive, when the Sacrifice of the Mediator [Mass] is offered for them, or when alms are given in the Church. But these things are of profit to those who, when they were alive, merited that they might afterward be able to be helped by these things, (On Faith Hope and Love, Chapter 110).

St. Augustine wrote these words eleven hundred years before Luther and kindred spirits broke off from Rome and eventually condemned as false the entire idea of Purgatory. While St. Augustine wrote these words nearly 400 years after Christ, he obviously believed his words represented concepts and practices directly handed down to the Church of his time from the very founders of our faith. Founders who themselves either knew Christ as he walked upon Earth or learned at the feet of those who did.

Let me add here just a bit to the discussion on this point of theology, as weak as it might be in comparison with Augustine or the Fathers. Let me refer to you a simple story which might demonstrate that we all, down deep, do believe in the reality of purgatory.

Why did Luther come to believe in the view that there is an 'Elect' that is saved, once-for-all? It seems our favorite German Monk was haunted by the realities of even his most mild sins and weaknesses. He spent hours in the confessional laying bare his soul before his fellow priests and yet often retained the fear he still was never good enough or pure enough to be accepted by God. Luther could never enjoy the comfort of knowing his sins had been forgiven.

In response to this fear, 'reformed' theologies such as Calvinism developed doctrines which taught that if you are one of God's Elect, then his grace is Irresistible, and you, as a saint, will be eternally Preserved in saving faith. They taught, addressing Luther's point, that one can have the 'assurance of salvation,' for if you find yourself believing in the Lord, you must have been Elected from all eternity to salvation, and there is nothing you or anyone else can do to cost you eternal bliss.

However, one of my best friends was an Evangelical. When we were in our 40's, he lost his grandmother. Like my grandmother and grandfather, she was a saintly woman, one he both loved and respected, one whose lifelong faith in Christ was an example to her family and friends.

A woman who my dear, dear friend anguished over. He told me as she grew to very old age and failing health, her attitudes changed. She, eventually, did and said things that made him wonder if she had forsaken Christ. When she died my friend feared his beloved grandmother was now tormented in the fires of hell. He believed that her later unbelief meant that she had never truly believed and had always been destined for the punishment of the reprobate.

How, he asked me on two occasions, can he know for sure she was saved?

The Catholic faith holds, "All who die in God's grace and friendship, but still imperfectly purified, are indeed assured of their eternal salvation, but after death they undergo purification so as to achieve the holiness necessary to enter the final joy of heaven."

The Church gives the name Purgatory to this final purification of the elect, which is entirely different from the punishment of the damned. (*Catechism of the Catholic Church* (*CCC*), Paragraph 1031).

We do not buy our way into heaven, and purgatory is not a second chance for non-believers. It is a place for my friend's grandmother, whom Jesus certainly wept over as her soul grew old and troubled, to go with assurance as to her ultimate reward in heaven. It is, truly, through the Catholic concept of purgatory that any man or woman can be assured of eventual salvation. For there is not one of us who doesn't stumble along the way, not one of us who can say we have maintained our faith and trust in the Lord perfectly throughout our entire lives. Are we then all, as my Evangelical friends like to say, 'backsliders,' and proven no longer part of the Elect? Do those who backslide never truly believe in the first place?

Or, did God provide for our imperfect souls – imperfect both in deed and in faith – a final refuge, a safety net to provide for our final purification?

About five years after this discussion with my friend, I was at a funeral; not for his grandmother, but for him. Dead, on his 46th birthday. Dead in his own mother's loving arms. He was no more or less perfect than I, or any of us. He believed, he sinned, he worked hard, he tried to do what was right and fair, he was obsessed with making his company work, he was the most loyal person I've ever met.

He died and did so far, far too early.

As I stood beside his casket at the wake a few days later, trying to not break down, trying not at the same moment to burst into laughter thinking about all his quirkiness and our thirty-year friendship, the one thing I knew for sure, with absolute, unquestioned, sure-as-I'm-standing-there, never-a-doubt-in-my-mind, certainty - this man was going to heaven. God willing, I will see him, and laugh with him, and talk football with him again. He might have enjoyed an express ride to heaven, or he might have spent some time in purgatory, but he, an Evangelical Christ-follower, would one day stand before our Lord.

The following day was horribly windy and cold as we stood around his grave site. The pastor of his Ft. Worth Evangelical mega-church stood before us and said the same thing he had said earlier that day before hundreds of well-wishers who came to the church to pay their respects. He said, as I paraphrase here, what I've heard every priest and every pastor say in those difficult moments:

"God, we thank you for all of your blessings. David Alan Corbin was a good man and a faithful servant of Christ. We ask you bless him and take him into your heaven to share in the eternal joy of your presence. We asked this in the name of the Lord, Jesus Christ."

To this we all said 'Amen.' Amen....we agree.

And we all did. As I've thought about those words since, I realized this was a Calvinist preacher with Calvinists followers uttering those 'amens.' But, following their theology, these prayers would be utterly useless. For, if the idea of Predestined Individual Election is correct, Dave was either part of the elect or not part of the elect and had been since the dawn of time. He either died believing and trusting in Christ, or he died in a state of unbelief. If he died in grace, he was already in heaven and all of our prayers were of no use. If he didn't, he was already suffering God's absence for eternity, and there was and is nothing our prayers can do to change his fate.

And yet, we all pray the same thing wherever there is a death. Maybe it's a human weakness and we are just saying these prayers with a teary wink, pretending for the grieving that we can in fact help the deceased. But, more likely, God will listen to our prayers for the dead as we all believe he listens when we pray for our fellow living human beings, or for the world at large.

I believe we are all lead by the Holy Spirit in those trying times to pray to God, for we all do understand we are all Christ's family and while we may believe Mother Teresa or Billy Graham might see God's glory at the very moment of their deaths, and Hitler and Stalin may be forever damned for their unbelief and sins, most of us sinners who believe in Jesus will someday share heaven with God. But we also know ourselves, our greed and lusts and coveting and anger. If we are honest, we would simply be embarrassed to stand immediately upon death before our Lord. We would repeat Peter's words in the boat early in his life with Christ, "Go away from me, Lord; I am a sinful man!' (Lk 5:8)

That is why there is purgatory. In many ways - as others have said - besides Christ's sacrifice, purgatory might be the most merciful and loving thing or process God has provided for us.

www.ingramcontent.com/pod-product-compliance
Lightning Source LLC
Chambersburg PA
CBHW011404010726
47495CB00009B/2775